Across the line . . .

Charger had a plan to breeze ahead of Lyle. He pulled his rocket booster lever. "Let's get charged!" he hollered. A blast of fire rumbled out of the back of his vehicle, and he sprang ahead of Car 606.

"Not so fast," Lyle growled. He yanked a lever in his own car. But instead of firing a rocket, he shot a grappling hook toward Charger. "One for my collection . . . ," he said with a nasty smirk.

The grappling hook plunged into one of the rear tires of Charger's car. *Blam!* The tire shredded.

Charger fought with his steering wheel as he struggled to keep control of Car 204. But it was no use—his vehicle skidded out. Right toward a thick concrete wall!

As Lyle shot past him in Car 606, Charger desperately threw his jump lever. Car 204's wings began to slide out. Charger rose into the sky, but he was too close to the wall. He couldn't clear it!

Car 204 almost sailed over the barrier, but then one of its wings clipped the edge—*skrraanggg!*— and was torn clean off. Charger's car spun through the air, tumbling over the wall.

Charger was flung back and forth as the car flipped. He braced himself as his racer fell toward the empty parking lot far, far below.

Collect all these awesome NASCAR Racers books!

NASCAR Racers: How They Work
NASCAR Racers: Official Owner's Manual
NASCAR Racers #2: Taking the Lead
NASCAR Racers #3: Tundra 2000

#1

THE

FAST LANE

J. E. BRIGHT

SCHOLASTIC INC.

New York Toronto London Auckland Sydney
Mexico City New Delhi Hong Kong

ISBN 0-439-24455-2

12 11 10 9 8 7 6 5 4 3 2 1   0 1 2 3 4 5/0

Printed in the U.S.A.   40

First Scholastic printing, September 2000

Cover illustration by Mel Grant
Designed by Susan Sanguily

1

VRROOOOOOOOMMMMMMMMMMM!

The heart-stopping roar of four finely tuned engines shook the ground. These engines weren't in any old, familiar racers. The four cars whipping down the brand-new track of Big River Raceway in New Motor City were the ultimate in high-tech . . . and high-speed. These cars—specially designed for NASCAR's new Unlimited Division—were capable of velocity and action nobody had ever seen before.

Car 204 was in the lead—tearing down the track at over 250 miles per hour. Mark McCutchen, better known as Charger, grimaced behind the wheel as he zoomed into a curve that tilted straight up, like he was driving on a wall. Totally sideways!

Lyle Owens in Car 606 and Carlos "Stunts" Rey in Car 404 were hot on Charger's bumper. Steve "Flyer" Sharp trailed slightly behind the other three in Car 808—but he was still shooting along so fast his vehicle was just a blur. Flyer shifted gears and started easing his racer past Lyle in Car 606.

Lyle wasn't about to let *that* happen. He swerved sharply, cutting Flyer off. But Lyle's swerve was too hard—he smacked into Car 404!

Inside Car 404, Stunts shook from the jolt. "Hey!" he cried. "You're messing up my hair!"

The four cars rushed onto a long straightaway, heading directly for the massive Motorsphere. The giant metal-and-glass globe loomed before them. Inside the huge sphere was the most amazing—and challenging—raceway ever built, and the four drivers couldn't wait to hit it.

Flyer was frustrated at having been cut off. He was losing ground to the others! "Time to show what this car can do," he decided.

"Wild blue yonder time," Flyer called as he threw the jump lever on his gearshift. Immediately, sleek metal wings slid out from the sides of his car. With an explosive blast, the jet booster fired from the back like a rocket. Car 808 launched into the air!

Flyer soared over the other cars, but he was headed straight toward the side of the Motorsphere.

He had to land—fast! Flyer flipped the jump lever off, and his wings retracted as he cruised back down toward the track.

Whammm! Inside Car 204, Charger flinched as his racer shuddered from a loud crash above him.

Flyer had bumped the top of Charger's car while he was landing!

Neither car was damaged, though. Flyer reached the track safely—and in the lead. He'd made it to the ground just in time to shoot into the Motorsphere entrance tunnel in front of the other cars.

The cars roared down the long passage that led into the spectacular sphere. They quickly shot out into the huge empty space inside the dome. Above the drivers was an impossibly huge track that arched and looped up to the super-high ceiling and dropped all the way to the bottom again like a roller coaster.

The cars shot across the vast floor of the Motorsphere without slowing down. The echoes of their engines bounced off the walls, filling the sphere with their thunder. When the four reached the far end of the dome, they hurtled right up the side, speeding along the curved wall of the globe . . . until they were racing upside down!

Stunts decided it was his turn to get some action going. "Let's get this show on the road!" he cried as he threw a lever beside his right hand. Car 404's forward jets erupted with flame, and Stunts blasted off

the wall—hurtling toward the floor of the Motorsphere!

His car tumbled end over end as it fell. Halfway to the ground, Stunts pulled his drogue chute lever. *Floop!* The chute—usually used to stop the car at the end of the race—popped out the back of the car and opened with a snap.

Car 404 slowed its deadly plunge as the drogue chute filled with air and acted as a parachute. Stunts drifted toward the ground.

With a smile, Stunts threw another lever that released the chute. It flapped away from his car and fluttered into the air. Car 404 dropped to the floor, wheels spinning full speed. With a screaming squeal Stunts took off down the track—way ahead of the other drivers. Awesome shortcut!

Meanwhile, Cars 808, 204, and 606 dashed down the curve of the ceiling, following the wall until they reached the ground right side up. Flyer, in Car 808, was a little ahead of the other two, which is why his car was the one that ran smack into Stunts's still-falling drogue chute.

Flyer hauled on the steering wheel, totally unable to see out his blocked windshield. Car 808 spun out. As it turned, the chute whipped off.

Car 204 and Car 606 whisked past Flyer, one on either side.

Stunts in Car 404 was the first one out of the Motorsphere, zooming down the track of Big River

Raceway. Charger in 204 and Lyle Owens in 606 followed him out soon after, both fighting for second place. Flyer chased them into the open air, but he was far behind.

Charger had a plan to breeze ahead of Lyle. He pulled his rocket booster lever. "Let's get charged!" he hollered. A blast of fire rumbled out of the back of his vehicle, and he sprang ahead of Car 606.

"Not so fast," Lyle growled. He yanked a lever in his own car. But instead of firing a rocket, he shot a grappling hook toward Charger. "One for my collection . . .," he said with a nasty smirk.

The grappling hook plunged into one of the rear tires of Charger's car. *Blam!* The tire shredded.

Charger fought with his steering wheel as he struggled to keep control of Car 204. But it was no use—his vehicle skidded out. Right toward a thick concrete wall!

As Lyle shot past him in Car 606, Charger desperately threw his jump lever. Car 204's wings began to slide out. Charger rose into the sky, but he was too close to the wall. He couldn't clear it!

Car 204 almost sailed over the barrier, but then one of its wings clipped the edge—*skrraanggg!*—and was torn clean off. Charger's car spun through the air, tumbling over the wall.

Charger was flung back and forth as the car flipped. Charger braced himself as his racer fell toward the empty parking lot far, far below.

2

Charger *plummeted toward the* hard ground. Calmly, he threw another lever. Then he let out an excited whoop as he exploded out of Car 204 in his Rescue Racer—a souped-up escape pod.

"Let's get charged!" Charger hollered as he pulled the Rescue Racer's glide lever. Little wings snapped out from either side of the emergency vehicle, slowing Charger's fall.

Below him, Car 204 smashed to the ground, shattering into pieces.

Inside the Rescue Racer, Charger activated his maneuvering jets. The escape pod had launched upside-down, but now with his jets firing, Charger began to glide right side up again.

He didn't get very far. Only a few seconds into his flip, the Rescue Racer stopped short. And hung motionless in midair!

"Hey!" Charger shouted. "Who put this thing in park?"

The other cars—closing in on the finish line—halted in their tracks, too, like someone had hit the pause button on a VCR. Then the Big River Raceway, the Motorsphere, New Motor City, and the whole background began to dissolve.

The scenery became fuzzier and fuzzier until it vanished in a flash of computer graphics!

The drivers were actually in the headquarters of the Fastex Corporation, inside the simulator room, surrounded by very expensive virtual reality equipment. Charger hung upside down in a racing simulator cockpit, wearing a VR helmet. The cockpit was designed to look like it was in a real race car, and the entire cage could move around to give the simulation a realistic feel.

Charger unbuckled his safety harness. He gave a startled yelp as he fell to the cold tile floor.

Next to him, Stunts and Flyer climbed out of their cockpits. "Hey!" Stunts called. "You can't stop now! I was about to win!"

The door to the high-tech room opened. In walked a pretty, athletic young woman named Megan

Fassler. She punched a few buttons on a hand-held computer. "The virtual reality simulator isn't a computer game," she reminded Stunts, giving her flame-red hair an impatient shake. "It's a training tool for a completely new form of NASCAR racing."

"Yeah," Stunts replied, "but I still would have won." He flashed her a grin, and his dark eyes twinkled beneath his mass of black hair.

Meanwhile, Charger had jumped over to Lyle's cockpit. As Lyle pulled off his helmet, Charger grabbed him by the front of his uniform.

"Hey!" Lyle protested.

Charger jerked him out of the cockpit. "You made me wreck, Owens!"

"Crybaby!" Lyle shot back.

Lyle broke free from Charger's hold and threw a punch. Charger ducked the swing and tackled Lyle to the floor.

Duck Dunaka, the husky, strong crew chief, pulled Lyle and Charger apart. "Break it up, you two," Duck demanded. "Who do you think you are—Cale Yarborough and Donnie Allison?"

Charger climbed to his feet. "He sent me into the wall, Mr. Dunaka!"

"Maybe a country boy like you just can't handle a supercar," Lyle taunted.

Instantly, Charger pulled back his hand to throw a punch at Lyle, but Duck grabbed him, holding him

back. "I'm a crew chief," Duck complained, "not a referee!"

"All right!" a forceful voice said from the doorway. "That's enough!"

Everyone turned slowly to face Jack Fassler. Jack was tall and commanding—and right now, obviously displeased. Jack owned Fastex Corporation, which had built New Motor City and sponsored Team Fastex. Jack was also Megan's father.

"I think we're all getting a little tired," Jack said pointedly. "Not to mention short-tempered. Let's call it a day."

Everyone began to walk toward the exit. "Wait a minute, Owens," Jack said. "I need to talk to you." Lyle turned around and waited while the others left.

When they were alone, Jack said, "I heard a rumor about you, but I didn't believe it."

"And what was that?" Lyle asked.

Jack frowned. "I heard they call you 'The Collector' because when you wreck another driver's car, you keep a piece of it . . . like a trophy."

Lyle faced Jack angrily. "It was just a simulation, Mr. Fassler," he said. "It's not the real thing—"

"I won't have a dirty driver on my team, Owens," Jack interrupted. He looked at Lyle evenly. "You're fired."

• • •

A few minutes later, Stunts, Flyer, and Charger walked out of the Fastex headquarters together, heading toward the parking lot. As they got close to Flyer's rugged, four-wheel-drive Jeep, Stunts nudged Flyer's shoulder.

"I hear you used to fly jets for the Air Force," Stunts said. "You want some real excitement, you should try racing *los motos*. You know—bikes." Stunts nodded toward his sleek Italian motorcycle, parked near the Jeep.

Flyer smiled at the challenge. "Wheels or wings, Stunts," he replied, "it's all one race to me."

Stunts climbed onto his motorcycle and looked at Charger. "Hey, *Señor* Famous Racing Family," he called. "Any of you McCutchens ever race bikes?"

"I can race anyone on anything," Charger answered confidently.

Stunts laughed. "You think you can race Carlos Rey, then you be at the diner tonight!" He revved his engine loudly. "Let's get this show on the road!" Stunts yelled. He popped a wheelie as he breezed away.

Charger grinned after Stunts and shook his head. At that moment, Lyle Owens stalked over. "Congratulations, McCutchen," he told Charger bitterly. "You just cost me my ride with Team Fastex."

Before Charger could reply, Lyle stormed past him and glided into a sinister-looking sports car.

Charger shrugged, and started toward his own

10

custom-made pickup truck. Before he could climb into the truck, though, an engine roared behind him. Tires squealed as Lyle peeled out.

At the last second, Lyle swerved his sports car—at Charger! Charger had to jump out of the way to avoid getting run down.

By the time Charger picked himself off the asphalt, Lyle was gone.

3

"**M**ark McCutchen," Jack Fassler said. "Charger."

Jack sat behind a large monitor in the Fastex Headquarters simulation room. On the screen was an ID picture of Charger, his chiseled, handsome face staring seriously into the camera.

"Racing's in his blood," Jack continued. "The McCutchen family has been in NASCAR for three generations."

He pressed a button on the keyboard in front of him, and the picture switched to Flyer's ID photo.

"Steve Sharp," Jack said. "Flyer. A fighter pilot— flew jets in combat."

Megan stepped closer to her father and put her hand on his shoulder. Jack pressed a key again, and the image changed to show Stunts's ID shot.

"Carlos Rey," Jack said. "Stunts. A natural driver. And a natural showman." He smiled as he looked at Stunts's cocky grin. "He reminds me of me, when I was that age."

Megan nodded. "Dad?" she asked carefully. "I think Lyle Owens deserves another chance."

Her father narrowed his eyes, and pressed another button on the keyboard. Lyle's photo popped up on the big screen. "You may have designed the cars, Megan," he replied, "but Team Fastex is mine." Jack quickly pressed the delete key, and the image of Lyle Owens dissolved. "And Team Fastex doesn't need a driver like The Collector."

Megan paced behind her father as he kept typing—and talking. "I've risked everything to get the NASCAR Unlimited Series started," Jack said. "To make it work, we need the best drivers in the—"

Suddenly, a video clip on the screen caught Jack's attention. "Look at this," he said. Megan peered over his shoulder.

On the monitor, a simulated racer was tearing up the track, spurting toward the checkered flag at the finish line. The car had the number 101 printed on it.

"This is a replay from the simulator's memory," Jack realized. "This driver has faster times than anybody on the team!" He took a closer look at the screen. "There's no name," he said. "Just an ID number."

"It was just to test the simulator—" Megan began.

"And he didn't want the team he's driving for now to know he was interested in the Unlimited Series," Jack interrupted. "Right?"

Megan bit her lip. "Dad, it's not—"

Jack turned to face her, his expression full of excitement. "The veteran drivers all say the super-cars are too 'experimental'," Jack said. "But maybe if we could get him to try out a real Unlimited Series car instead of the simulation—"

"I'm not sure you'd want this driver," Megan broke in.

"I'll tell you what I want, Megan," Jack replied. He pointed at the monitor. "I want that man driving for Fastex."

Megan looked down at her feet. "Like you say, Dad," she said, lifting her head. She had a sour look on her face. "Team Fastex is all yours."

The headquarters of the Rexcor Corporation was a tall, gleaming, black slab of a building. An enormous Rexcor logo covered a big piece of the sinister skyscraper's side.

On the top floor was Garner Rexton's immense office. Garner was the president of Rexcor, and he did not seem to be in a good mood as he glowered behind his vast desk. Across from Garner, looking nervous, was Lyle Owens.

"I'm paying you a lot of money to spy on Team

Fastex," Garner growled. "That won't be easy, will it? Now that you've gotten yourself fired."

Lyle sat up straight in his chair. "It's not my fault, Mr. Rexton," he explained. "It was that Charger McCutchen—he's got it in for me."

Garner crossed his arms over his chest.

Lyle swallowed. "I was getting friendly with Fassler's daughter, Megan," he continued quickly. "She knows those cars better than her father does."

For a long moment, Garner just stared at Lyle in silence.

Finally, Lyle couldn't take the silence any longer. "Uh, Mr. Rexton?" he began. "I was thinking—since I need a ride, maybe I could drive for Rexcor—"

"I have to know everything about Team Fastex," Garner interrupted. "Everything about their cars. I'm not just going to beat Jack Fassler . . ."

Garner Rexton's eyes filled with a determined, vicious gleam.

"I'm going to destroy him," Garner said. He smiled at Lyle, and Lyle felt a chill run down to his toes. "Now go back to Fastex," he finished, "and find out how I can do it."

The diner's neon sign glowed against the night sky. The restaurant was on a lonely highway far from town, and it was a hangout for motorcycle racers, hot-rodders, and drag racers. The diner owned a

long, abandoned road nearby that drivers used for casual competition.

The rumble of motorcycle engines idling shook the diner's parking lot. Charger and Stunts were sitting on two of the cycles, but another bike beside them had no driver. That was because Flyer was standing next to his Jeep, with his helmet in his hand. Perched in his Jeep, his pretty girlfriend Glorie glared at Flyer unhappily.

"Come on, Flyer!" Charger called.

Stunts shook his head. "I couldn't have a steady girlfriend," he told Charger. "Wouldn't be fair to all the other girls."

Flyer ignored them, and kept his gaze on Glorie's face.

"I can't take the waiting, Sharp," Glorie told Flyer.

"This won't take long," Flyer replied. "We're just racing to the quarry and back—"

"I'm not just talking about tonight!" Glorie broke in. She slid down from the Jeep's high seat. "You've got no business racing, Sharp! What if you have another one of those . . . those *things*—"

"Shh!" Flyer said, glancing around to make sure nobody had overheard. "Not here, Glorie." Behind him, Stunts and Charger revved their engines impatiently. "They're waiting for me," Flyer said to Glorie. "I have to go."

Flyer turned around and hurried over to his motorcycle.

Stunts revved his engine again and popped a wheelie as he sped off. Flyer and Charger followed him out of the parking lot, down a dark road away from the diner.

Glorie was left alone standing beside Flyer's Jeep. She watched Flyer race off as though she might never see him again.

4

The woods were dark and deep. Silvery moonlight bathed the trees in an eerie glow. The gentle sound of frogs echoed through the forest. Then . . .

Rrrrrrrrooooooaaaaaaaarrrrr!

Stunts, Flyer, and Charger blasted down a dark road through the woods on their motorcycles. Their headlights cut through the darkness.

The bike racers leaned into an S-shaped curve, and then flowed into a straightaway. Stunts accelerated, scurrying past Flyer and Charger. As Stunts crested a hill, his cycle left the road for a moment, flying through the air. He landed again quickly, his tires squealing.

Flyer and Charger followed a second later,

launching off the ground and landing again just like Stunts had.

In front of Stunts was a terrifyingly sharp turn. He slowed slightly—his brake light flashing red. Stunts took the turn easily.

Behind him, Flyer and Charger pressed their brakes as they entered the turn, too. Charger whisked through the curve, but Flyer's rear tire slipped.

Flyer slid off the road, skidding in the gravel alongside. He barely managed to stay upright as Charger shot on ahead.

Stopping his cycle for a second, Flyer inhaled deeply. He held his hands out in front of him, checking them out. They weren't shaking.

"I'm all right," Flyer said nervously. "Just an accident."

He revved his engine and cruised after Stunts and Charger.

Stunts was still blasting down the road, with Charger roaring closer, catching up. They both sizzled around a curve.

As Stunts came out of the turn, a sudden flash of car headlights blinded him. A car was coming from the other direction!

A horrible squeal came from the car as the driver slammed on his brakes. The car skidded sideways, off the road. *Crraaang!* It banged into a tree, crumpling its fender.

Stunts's heart skipped a beat as he swerved past the car. He barely missed colliding with it. Charger slid to a panicked stop, gravel kicking up from his tires.

A few feet down the road, Stunts pulled over. He glanced back at Charger. "Hey!" he called. "You all right, man?"

Charger nodded, but quickly turned his attention to the driver of the car, who was climbing out. "This is a private road!" Charger hollered at the driver. "It's a closed course! Didn't you see the signs?"

The driver shook his head. "No, no," he said. "I am called Diesel, Diesel Spitz. I am not from your country. The English on the sign—it was not meaning so clear enough, I think."

Rrrrrroooooaaaaarrrrrrrrrr!

Stunts's eyes widened as he heard the approaching motorcycle. "Flyer!" he yelled.

Flyer whipped around the corner on his cycle, blinding Charger, Stunts, and Diesel with his headlight. As soon as Flyer spotted the crashed car and Charger's bike in the middle of the road, he hit his brakes frantically. But he was going too fast for a clean stop. Flyer's motorcycle skidded wildly, and his back tire fishtailed, kicking up off the ground.

The out-of-control bike flung Flyer into the air. Then the driverless motorcycle shot off the side of the road. It smashed into a thick tree and was still.

Once again, the dark forest was silent.

5

*T*he parking lot of the diner had filled up with cars since the three guys had raced off into the woods.

Glorie was still waiting in Flyer's Jeep. *Rrrrrmmmm!* The sound of a car approaching made her sit up and peer out the windshield. As it came into view, Glorie gasped.

Diesel's car roared up the road to the diner. Its fender was banged up, and as the vehicle pulled to a stop in the lot, Glorie could see Flyer's crumpled, totally wrecked motorcycle tied to the rear bumper. Her heart stopped.

Glorie clambered out of the Jeep and rushed toward the new arrival. "Sharp!" she shouted.

Diesel climbed out of the car. When she saw he

was alone, Glorie stopped short. She covered her mouth with her hand, fearing the worst.

Vrrrrrrrrrooooommmmm!

The chainsaw sound of two motorcycles approaching made Glorie glance down the road. A pair of headlights flickered into view.

Glorie breathed a deep sigh of relief. Stunts and Charger drove up the street. Flyer was riding double behind Stunts. As they came closer, Glorie noticed that Flyer was covered with a film of mud and pond slime.

When the cycles pulled to a stop, Flyer quickly dismounted and hurried over to Glorie. He smiled. "I told you I wouldn't be gone long," he said.

"What happened?" Glorie asked. She looked him up and down to make sure he wasn't hurt.

"Flyer took a little flight—" Stunts called over from his bike.

"And landed in a swamp!" Charger added.

Stunts barked a short laugh, and then he and Charger cracked up.

Glorie didn't think the situation was funny at all. She turned around and stalked away.

"Glorie!" Flyer called. "Hey! Wait a minute!"

But Glorie was furious. She climbed into the Jeep, slammed the door, and started the engine.

"Come on, Glorie," Flyer begged. "That's my Jeep!"

Glorie ignored him. She didn't even glance at

Flyer as she drove across the parking lot. The Jeep's tires squealed as Glorie took off down the road.

Flyer gazed after his girlfriend, feeling helpless.

"*Oye*, Flyer," Stunts said. "You need a ride." He grinned as Flyer turned to face him. "Or are you gonna *fly* home?"

Charger smiled at Flyer, who was still soaking wet. "Maybe he's gonna swim," Charger suggested.

Again, Charger and Stunts broke into laughter.

Flyer shook his head for a moment.

But then he started laughing, too.

The next day, Charger's pickup truck rumbled into an access tunnel—the entrance to Big River Raceway's paved infield. As the truck drove out of the tunnel, it made a screeching turn. Charger headed across the empty infield toward the gleaming silver Team Fastex hauler, which was parked near the track.

Charger pulled up beside Flyer's Jeep—which he must have gotten back from Glorie. Next to the Jeep was Stunts's motorcycle and Jack Fassler's exotic sports car. As soon as the truck stopped, Charger jumped out. His ten-year-old brother, Miles McCutchen, climbed down from the passenger side.

Miles was wearing a cap turned backward on his head, but other than that he looked just like Charger—only smaller.

"This is big-time racing, Miles," Charger said. "Team Fastex! And I don't want them to know I have to baby-sit my kid brother."

"Come on, Charger," Miles argued. "I could be a big help on the team. I know everything about cars . . ." He paused a moment, and smiled. "Well, except how to drive one."

Charger returned his little brother's smile, and then yanked Miles's cap off his head. He turned the cap around and put it back on Miles's head again, pushing the brim down over his eyes. "I'll let you come in later and meet the guys," Charger said. "Okay?"

As Miles pulled the cap off again, Charger started walking toward the hauler. "Just try to stay out of trouble for a while!" Charger shouted over his shoulder.

Miles stood there a moment, unsure what to do. "I'll go get a Frozen Whizzie," he decided, putting his cap back on as Charger disappeared into the hauler. Miles turned the bill backward with a defiant flourish.

"I'll be a better driver than him, too," Miles whispered to himself. "Just as soon as I can see over the dashboard."

Charger entered the Team Fastex hauler and walked over to stand next to Flyer and Stunts. Jack had already begun giving them a tour. "The Team Fastex

hauler has one of the most advanced communications systems in the world," Jack explained. He waved his hand at a bank of blinking lights and radar displays on monitors. "My daughter Megan designed it herself."

Then Jack led the team into the ready room, which was a small but comfortable-looking lounge with four lockers along one wall. Three of the lockers had names printed on them: STUNTS, FLYER, and CHARGER. The fourth locker was blank.

Jack nodded toward the lockers. "The ready room is a home-away-from-home for the team," he said, "with everything a driver needs."

Stunts reached over to open his locker. "Everything I need?" he asked. "Then there must be some good-looking *chicas* living in my locker—"

He opened the slim metal door. *Sproing!* Stunts's Team Fastex racing suit popped out like it was attacking him. Stunts yelped and fell backward.

"The lockers are spring-loaded," Jack said. "So you can change racing suits in a hurry."

Flyer opened his locker. *Sproing!* His racing suit flung out, but he was ready for it. Flyer caught the suit with one hand. Excellent reflexes.

Charger stepped over to peer down at Stunts, who was still lying on the floor. "This is my color, man," Stunts said. "I'm gonna look *good*."

"You don't need a racing suit to sit in a simulator," Charger pointed out. He turned to look at Jack.

"When are we going to get to drive the real thing, Mr. Fassler?" he asked.

"Sooner than you think," Jack answered. At that, he walked out of the ready room.

The moment Jack left, the floor started to shake.

Charger glanced around with a puzzled expression.

"Do you feel that?" Stunts asked. "It's like an earthquake!"

"What is it?" Charger asked.

Flyer glanced at the watercooler on the other side of the room. The water in the fat bottle was vibrating and rippling. A big smile lit up Flyer's face.

"It's the real deal," Flyer said.

6

*T*he guys quickly pulled on their Team Fastex uniforms. Then they rushed out of the hauler, still zipping up their suits. They hurried over to the pit wall.

Vrroooooooommmmmmmmmmm!

Charger's mouth dropped open as he got his first look at a real NASCAR Unlimited Series racer. It blazed by, hurtling down the track in a blur. Charger thought it was the most beautiful thing he'd ever seen in his life.

Duck Dunaka was standing near the hauler when Jack found him. "You should've told me that new driver was here," Jack told Duck grumpily.

Duck shrugged. "Megan wanted it to be a surprise," he said.

"Where is Megan, anyway?" Jack asked. He

peered around, but he didn't see any sign of his daughter.

"She'll turn up," Duck replied. "Somewhere."

Jack nodded. "I'm sure she will," he said. "Duck, I think it's time for you to go get our surprise ready." A smile crept over his usually stern features. "And I'll go get the guys."

After giving Duck a few minutes of lead time, Jack walked over to where Charger, Stunts, and Flyer were still staring open-mouthed at the car shattering speed records on the track. Jack stood behind the drivers and cleared his throat. "You think you're good enough to catch a NASCAR veteran?" he asked.

The three Team Fastex drivers whirled eagerly to face their boss.

Bbbrrrrrrrrrooooooooooaaaaaaarrrrrr!

This time, the engine roar hadn't come from the track. Charger, Stunts, and Flyer turned to find the source of the loud, vibrating sound.

Next to the Fastex hauler, three Unlimited Series cars were parked. Duck had started one.

Stunts's eyes grew very wide. "Awesome-issimo, man!" he shouted over the deafening roar. "Just like me! That one must be mine!"

"And the one in the middle's mine!" Flyer said. "I know because it looks just like my dreams! It's like when I first got my wings."

Charger couldn't take his eyes off the car on the

left. A big 204 was printed on the side. "My dad used to race number 204," Charger said quietly.

Duck opened the door of Stunts's car and stuck his head out. *Bbbvvvvvrroooooooommmmm!* He revved the accelerator. "The cars sound ready, Jack!" he called over.

Behind the three drivers, the car on the track whipped by.

Jack nodded his head toward the speeding car, which was already vanishing into the distance of Big River Raceway. "I think he just lapped you," Jack said.

For a second, Stunts, Flyer, and Charger were too stunned to move. They glanced at one another, unsure what to do. Then Stunts let out a wild whoop and the three drivers dashed for the cars like kids running toward presents under a Christmas tree. Jack smiled as they raced past him.

Flyer was the first to reach his car. He jumped nimbly into his cockpit.

As Charger was climbing into his own car, Stunts vaulted up on top of it to get to his. He ran a few steps across Charger's hood before jumping into his car.

"Hey!" Charger yelled. "Don't scratch my paint!"

Duck shook his head. "Rookies," he said, rolling his eyes.

Inside his car, Flyer pulled on his racing helmet. Then he pressed the starter button on the dashboard. Automatically, his safety harness slid out from the seat and closed around him.

Flyer was the first to take off down pit road, with Stunts and Charger following him a split-second later. Just as the car already whizzing down the track passed Flyer again, he veered onto Big River Raceway and erupted after the driver ahead of him, his tires squealing. Stunts and Charger stayed hot on his heels.

Jack and Duck watched from behind the pit wall. "That Charger reminds me of his dad," Duck said. "And his grandfather, too—old Mack McCutchen."

"I couldn't let a child of mine drive," Jack said. "Racing's too hard on you, physically and emotionally. I'm glad Megan isn't interested."

Duck glanced at Jack. His lips were pressed tightly shut.

Behind Jack and Duck—unseen by them both—Lyle Owens appeared from behind the hauler. After glancing around to make sure nobody had spotted him, Lyle slipped inside.

Lyle headed right for the main computer. He pulled a floppy disk out of his pocket, and slipped it into the disk drive. He raised his head to look around once more.

Then he pressed the ENTER key.

Meanwhile, Flyer was still trying to catch up to the mystery car ahead of him, with Charger closing behind.

Charger put his hand on the gearshift. "Let's see

what the real thing feels like!" he said. He threw the lever on his forward rockets.

With a blast of fire, Charger's car accelerated to an almost impossible speed. He launched past Flyer, shooting ahead of him.

Flyer's eyes narrowed. He pulled his jump lever. Wings slid out from the sides of his car and his turbojet exploded with flame. Immediately, Flyer's car rose into the air and soared over Charger's car.

But something was wrong with Flyer. His heart was thumping too fast in his chest and he started breathing hard. His face broke out in a hot sweat. Flyer lifted one hand off the steering wheel—it was shaking violently.

"No . . ." Flyer moaned. Desperately, he hit the jump lever again, turning off his turbo engines. His car slowed in the air, and drifted back to land behind Charger's car.

Flyer gasped for breath. He slowed his car to a stop. "Why is this happening to me?" Flyer asked out loud.

Then Flyer set his jaw, crinkling his eyes in determination. "I'm not going to let it beat me," he swore. He grabbed the steering wheel with both hands and stomped on the accelerator.

Flyer took off down Big River Raceway once more, fishtailing slightly as he picked up speed. His tires squealed.

Flyer wasn't going to give up.

7

*J*ack could only see a partial view of the track from where he was standing behind the pit wall. "I'm going up in the tower for a better look," he told Duck.

A minute or so after Jack had walked away, Duck remembered something—something important. "Jack!" he called.

The owner of Team Fastex had just opened the door to the hauler. Jack turned back around to face the crew chief.

Duck hurried over. "I'm not gonna let 'em run for very long," Duck said, tilting his head toward the cars blasting past behind him. "Those new forced combustion carbs could start to overheat."

Jack gripped the edge of the door. "It's not a safety risk, Duck," he insisted. "The heat sensors will shut the engines down before they become explosive."

Lyle Owens was hiding right behind the door. His eyes widened as he heard the word "explosive." *Very* interesting!

"The heat sensors are new," Duck replied to Jack. "I don't trust them."

"I guess that's worth checking out," Jack said. He turned around to shut the hauler's door—and came face to face with Lyle Owens. Jack's mouth dropped open in surprise. "What are you doing here?" he demanded.

Lyle walked out of the shadow behind the door. He smiled innocently. "I just wanted to tell you, Mr. Fassler," he said smoothly, "that I'm going to be driving for Team Rexcor."

Without waiting for a reply from Jack or Duck, Lyle hurried out of the hauler and strode away.

Jack stared after Lyle, a puzzled expression on his face. But the confused look quickly turned to suspicion. He didn't trust that Lyle Owens—not at all.

Duck pulled out a small hand-held radio. It squawked as he turned it on. "Listen," he told one of the drivers, "bring it into the pits next time around."

The mystery driver's car blazed down the track, headed into a straightaway. Charger and Stunts quickly followed. But the mystery driver slowed down and pulled off onto pit road as Charger and Stunts kept zooming along.

33

Jack watched the mystery driver coming into the pits. "You can tell he's experienced just from the way he handles the car," he noted.

Duck gave a little cough. "Um," he said, "I think I'll go grind a carb." With that, Duck walked quickly away from Jack.

"What's gotten into him?" Jack wondered.

The mystery driver eased up onto an IMP unit in the pits. The IMP unit—which stood for Independently Mobile Pit unit—was a high-tech garage on wheels. During an off-track race, it could even be driven onto a road for a rolling pit stop. But most of the time it was parked in the pits and the racers drove up onto it like it was an automotive aircraft carrier.

As soon as the car had come to a stop, one of the IMP's mechanical arms reached out and automatically began filling the gas tank.

Jack climbed up onto the IMP next to the mystery driver's car. The driver climbed out, still wearing a racing helmet.

"Hi," Jack greeted the driver. "I'm Jack Fassler. It's a pleasure to meet—"

He cut off his words as the driver pulled off the helmet, revealing flame-red hair.

Jack's heart skipped a beat.

The mystery driver was his daughter.

"Megan!" Jack exclaimed.

"Hi, Dad," Megan said. She looked a little nervous,

but she gathered up her courage and looked her father in his eyes. "You know those lap times you were so impressed by on the simulator? Those were *mine.*"

Jack shook his head in disbelief, not knowing what to say.

"I'm the driver you want on Team Fastex," Megan said.

8

*T*he *Motorsphere looked even* larger and more intimidating than it had seemed in the simulation.

Charger tried not to stare up at it through his windshield as he hurtled toward the entrance tunnel of the giant sphere. He had to stay focused, even though the globe was truly imposing. Charger knew that it would take all his driving skill to master the Motorsphere—it was a track unlike any ever built before.

The echo of Charger's engine bounced off the walls of the tunnel, ringing in his ears. Stunts was hot on Charger's heels, making the howl in the tunnel twice as loud.

Both cars shot out onto the wide-open floor of the vast dome. Charger thought that the sight of the looping racetrack overhead was a billion times more thrilling than the same view in the simulation. Nothing could fake the sensation of really driving across the colossal sphere.

Stunts chased Charger along the track that covered the whole length of the dome. He, too, felt a sense of total awe as the track began to tilt upward. Excitement hammered in his chest as he sped up the curved wall toward the top of the dome.

About the same time that Flyer finally reached the entrance tunnel to the Motorsphere, Miles McCutchen stood near a gate in a fence by the sphere's exit tunnel. Miles slurped his cold, fruity Frozen Whizzie through a straw.

Charger's little brother looked around. "I don't hear the cars anymore," Miles said, his voice full of disappointment. He squashed his backward cap further onto his head. "Way bummer—I missed all the action because I was getting a stupid Frozen Whizzie!"

Miles walked through the gate, shaking his drink to mix up the blended ice. He wandered over to the edge of the track, and glanced around again. Not a car in sight.

With a shrug, Miles jumped down onto the track and headed toward the infield. Heat rippled off the asphalt in the bright sunlight.

About halfway across the track, Miles slurped on his Frozen Whizzie again. The straw sucked up only

air, so Miles stopped to open up the lid of his cup. He sloshed around the little that was left.

Vvvvvrrrrrrrrooooooooooooooaaaaaaaarrrr!

Miles turned around to see what was making that huge, echoing roar behind him. He was standing in the middle of the track, a few yards away from the exit tunnel.

Charger's car spouted out of the tunnel, with Stunts right on his bumper.

They were headed right for Miles!

Miles's eyes nearly bugged out of his head. He dropped his Frozen Whizzie cup in shock.

Charger saw his little brother ahead of him instantly. His stomach lurched. "Miles!" he hollered. He slammed on his brakes.

The tires of Charger's car let out a piercing squeal. Smoke billowed into the air from the scorched rubber. Charger spun out—smashing into the side of Stunts's car.

"Hey!" Stunts shouted as Charger banged into his flank.

Without thinking, Stunts flipped his maneuvering jets lever.

Along one side of Stunts's car, rocket boosters blasted—propelling the car up onto two wheels.

Inside Charger's car, the world spun crazily. All Charger could hear was the shriek of his tires. He hoped against hope that his car had somehow missed his little brother.

Charger's car was totally out of control, spinning toward the concrete wall. He fought with the steering wheel for a long, desperate moment before he realized that there was nothing he could do. Charger hit his escape pod lever.

Fooom!

Charger's Rescue Racer ejected out the top a half-second before the car hurtled into the wall. Behind Charger, his car crumpled, totaled.

Miles hadn't moved from his spot. He stared—terrified—as Stunts's car soared past him. The two wheels of the car that were in the air nearly grazed Miles's head as it rumbled past him.

Whaaaaammmmm!

Charger's Rescue Racer escape pod crashed onto the track upside-down—only a few feet from where Miles was standing.

"Charger!" Miles screamed.

Behind him, Stunts's car flopped down on all four wheels again with a bounce. It skidded to a screeching stop.

Miles stumbled over to Charger's Rescue Racer. He kneeled beside it and peered inside. "Are you all right, Charger?" he asked. His voice shook with fear.

But before Charger could answer—

Vvvvvrrrrrrrrrooooooooooooooooaaaaaaaarrrr!

Miles glanced toward the Motorsphere tunnel exit. His eyes were as wide as hubcaps.

Flyer's car gushed out of the tunnel.

"Oh, no," Miles whispered.

Because he had been so far behind, Flyer had his pedal to the metal. The speed of his car was unbelievable.

To Miles, Flyer's car looked like a missile— heading their way!

9

*C*harger *scrambled out of his*
Rescue Racer.

"Charger!" Miles screamed again. Flyer's car was bearing down on Miles and Charger at almost 300 miles per hour.

The second that Flyer saw the mess on the track ahead of him, he lunged for his jump lever and slammed it. His wings shot out from the sides of his car and he began to sail into the air.

Charger quickly pulled himself into a crouch and leaped at his little brother, tackling him to the ground.

From his sprawled position on the track, Miles looked up to see Flyer's car soaring overhead—only inches from his nose.

Vvvvvrrrrrrrrrroooooooooooommmmmmm!

The roar was deafening. Miles had wanted to be close to the new Unlimited Series cars, but this was way more than he had bargained for!

Flyer's car landed a few feet away from the brothers, and quickly skidded to a halt.

Still lying on the track, Miles and Charger met each other's shocked eyes. "I'm sorry I made you wreck, Charger," Miles whispered.

Charger began to pull himself to his knees. "It's okay, Miles," he said wearily. "You didn't know we'd be racing today. I didn't know myself until a little while ago."

Miles sat up, and Charger reached over to ruffle his little brother's hair. "Hey," Charger said, "where's your cap?"

Both brothers turned around to look at Flyer's car.

Miles's cap was stuck in Flyer's radiator grille.

Talk about a close call!

A little while later, Miles sat on a metal stool near the IMP, watching Charger's battered car being raised up on a hydraulic lift. Duck was overseeing the operation.

"I wasn't scared at all, Mr. Dunaka," Miles told Duck. "Well, maybe just a little . . . but not really *scared* scared. If you know what I mean."

"Uh-huh," Duck said. He held up a roll of gray duct tape. "Hey, kid, I think they're cheating us on

this duck tape." Duck always called duct tape *duck* tape—which was how he got his nickname. He tossed the big roll to Miles. "See if there's really two hundred yards on this roll."

A big smile crossed Miles's face as he jumped off his stool. "You bet, Duck!" he said. "Anything you need help with, you just ask!"

On the other side of the IMP, Charger stood by Megan as she controlled a mechanical arm to lower an engine into a test car. The car was a skeleton of a finished Unlimited Series racer—completely stripped down.

Stunts sauntered up to them. "*Oye*, Megan," he said, "I hear your papa doesn't want you to drive for the team."

Megan didn't look up at Stunts. She kept her attention focused on moving the mechanical arm. "He hasn't decided yet," she replied. Then Megan pulled a lever—much harder than she needed to pull it.

With a groan, Megan turned around, and found Stunts standing right behind her.

"You wanna go for a ride," Stunts said with a smile, "you can borrow my car anytime."

Megan didn't say anything for a long moment. Instead she stared coldly at Stunts. "I *built* your car," she said finally.

Then she noticed Flyer heading for the hauler.

"Flyer!" she called out. Megan hurried after him, leaving Stunts and Charger by the IMP.

Stunts winked at Charger. "I like those brainy *chicas*," he said. "They've got earning potential. Yeah, if there's anything I like, it's a *chica* who can make me some money."

Charger just rolled his eyes.

By the time Megan caught up with Flyer, he was already sitting in front of a computer terminal in the hauler. Flyer looked up as Megan stopped beside him.

"There's some video I want you to see," Megan said. "You've noticed the tall tower on the hauler, right? Well, that observation tower has computer controlled cameras that follow every Team Fastex car."

She picked up a remote control and turned on a large video screen on one wall. The image on the screen showed Flyer's car zipping around the main track of Big River Raceway.

"We also have cameras installed in every car," she added.

Megan pressed a button on the remote and the picture shifted to show Flyer hitting his jump lever. For a second Flyer thought she was showing the scene when he'd jumped over Miles and Charger. But no. It was a video of the moment when he had

tried to pass Charger's car by jumping over it. The moment when Flyer had . . . He didn't want to finish the thought.

But the video showed him what he'd been trying to avoid thinking about. The cameras had clearly captured him sailing through the air—and the panicked look on his face. In the replay, his forehead was covered with sweat and it was clear that he was having trouble breathing as he raised his shaking hands and stared at them.

"No . . ." the video image of Flyer whispered—and turned off his turbojet boosters.

In the hauler, Flyer looked down at his feet. He couldn't stand watching himself having the bizarre attack. The attacks were something he couldn't understand . . . and couldn't control.

Megan kept the video running. In it, Flyer asked himself, "Why is this happening to me?"

Flyer glanced up just in time to catch a look of determination cross his face in the video. Flyer remembered how, moments later, he had grabbed the steering wheel and squealed down the track again.

With the remote, Megan clicked the video screen off. She met Flyer's eyes.

"Have you told anybody else about this?" Flyer asked her.

"What should I tell them?" Megan replied with concern in her voice. "What happened to you out there?"

Flyer narrowed his eyes. "Whatever it was, I can handle it," he answered. "By *myself*."

With that, Flyer stood up and stormed past Megan toward the door.

"Sharp!" Megan called after him.

Flyer stopped. He glanced back at her.

"You're *not* by yourself," she told him firmly. "You're part of Team Fastex. And I'm not going to let you do anything to hurt the team."

"I can race, Megan," Flyer said. "I have to."

Megan shrugged. "It's not your decision," she said.

Flyer stared at her for a second, worry and anger flickering on his face. Then he wheeled around and stalked out the door of the hauler.

After he'd left, Megan slumped into the seat in front of the computer, shaking her head.

"It's *my* decision now," she said.

Meanwhile, Miles was busy on pit road.

He had stuck a piece of duct tape by the IMP, and had walked backward several hundred feet, unspooling the tape as he went.

"A hundred and eighty-seven yards . . ." Miles counted, "a hundred eighty-eight yards . . . a hundred eighty-nine yards . . ."

10

*J*ack was having a very unpleasant meeting at the bank.

He'd gone over to the EnormaBanc building early the next morning to talk about the huge loans he'd taken out in order to build New Motor City and Team Fastex. But the talks were not going well.

"I'm sorry, Mr. Fassler," a bank officer told Jack. "If it were just me, I'd be willing to put off your next loan payment."

Jack tried to smile at the man across the desk, but it just came out as a grimace. "The first Unlimited Series race is next week," Jack explained. "As soon as we start winning races—"

"The bank has been sold, Mr. Fassler," the officer interrupted. "The new owner will want to review all our major loans. And your loan is definitely considered major."

Jack cocked his head. "Who's the new owner?" he asked.

Outside the bank tower, workmen scrambled up ladders, prying off the old EnormaBanc logo over the entranceway. They lowered the logo—which was a big globe with a dollar sign in the middle—to the sidewalk.

The new logo was on the ground, leaning on the building. It was covered with a tarp, waiting to be hoisted into place.

A workman walked over to the new logo and whipped off the tarp.

If Jack had been outside, his blood would have run cold.

The new logo was a design around the word REXCOR.

Jack Fassler had spent an incredible amount of money to build the best NASCAR track in the world.

And now he owed it all to Garner Rexton.

That same sinister Rexcor logo hung above the doorway of a dark, windowless garage on the other side of town.

Lyle Owens drove his sports car up to the garage and parked outside.

Inside, the first thing he saw was a line of racing

cars. They looked very similar to the Team Fastex racers, but there was something nastier about them—something menacing that Lyle liked.

At the end of the row of cars was a weight bench. Sitting on the bench was a totally buff, beautiful woman with dark black hair. She was doing bicep curls with a set of dumbbells.

Lyle walked up to her. "Hi," he said. "I'm Lyle Owens. Do you know where I can find the Team Rexcor drivers?"

The woman shot Lyle an angry look. "I'm Zorina," she said, "and *I'm* a Team Rexcor driver."

Zorina tossed the dumbbells to Lyle. He caught them, staggering backward under their weight.

Grabbing a towel, Zorina stood up. She wiped her face and glared at Lyle. "I was racing speedboats and off-road bikes before I ever started modeling," she told him.

Lyle was still struggling with the dumbbells as Zorina stalked toward him. He might have fallen backward, but someone caught him from behind.

Zorina stared right into Lyle's eyes. "This is not just another pretty face, baby," she sneered. Then she grabbed the dumbbells out of his hands, and walked away.

Whoever had caught Lyle pushed him roughly to his feet. Lyle turned around to face him.

"I am Diesel Spitz," the guy said. "I was being the top-rated driver in Europe—"

A burly guy stepped out from behind Diesel, interrupting him. "Until he started wrecking every car he drove," the burly man finished for Diesel. "That's why they call him Junker."

Diesel sneered at the burly guy. "I will show you who is junk, Hondo Hines," he hissed. He turned back to Lyle. "Both of you," Diesel said dangerously. Then he stomped out of the garage.

Lyle shook his head and looked at Hondo. "What do they call you?" Lyle asked.

"They call me Specter," Hondo replied. "I wreck *other* people's cars—not my own."

Crang!

A crunch of metal filled the garage. Lyle looked over and saw that Diesel had come back into the workshop carrying a sledgehammer, and had started smashing a junk car.

Diesel bellowed with rage and walloped the junk car again.

"Welcome to Team Rexcor, Mr. Owens," said the voice of Garner Rexton.

Lyle whirled around, expecting to find Garner standing behind him. But instead he saw something very peculiar.

A thing that looked vaguely like a man and more like a machine stood in the middle of the garage. The robot had tools hanging all over him and parts of his body were pieces of high-tech equipment. In

the center of his chest was a video screen with an image of Garner's face on it.

"My name is Spex," the strange creature said in a metallic voice. "I'm the Rexcor crew chief."

"Nice to meet you," Lyle said. He offered his hand for Spex to shake. Spex stuck out the chunk of machinery his hand was made of, and Lyle withdrew his own nervously.

On the video screen, Garner Rexton cleared his throat. "Were you able to find out anything useful about Team Fastex?" Garner asked Lyle.

"Uh, yes, sir, Mr. Rexton," Lyle replied. "I copied the files on their forced combustion carburetors."

"Well?" Garner demanded. "Where are they?"

Lyle pulled a disk out of his pocket.

Spex held out his arm toward Lyle. "Put the disk in my hand," the robot demanded. Lyle looked closely at Spex's hand, and sure enough, there was a disk drive embedded in his palm.

Lyle quickly slid the disk into the slot. It clicked into place.

"They're having trouble with their engines overheating," Lyle reported.

As Garner looked over the data, Lyle thought that Team Rexcor was the oddest, scariest group of drivers and crew he'd ever seen in his life.

Even more strange, though, was how much Lyle felt like he belonged.

51

11

Megan *whipped down the Big River Raceway* track in the test car she'd finished working on a little while earlier. She glanced at the temperature gauge. "The temperature's past the red line, Duck," she reported.

Duck stood near the Team Fastex hauler in the pit, holding the radio.

"I'm going to try to shut the engine down," Megan continued.

Jack had just entered Big River Raceway. He pulled up beside the hauler and climbed out.

Inside the speeding test car, Megan reached for the ignition button. "Ignition off," she said. Megan pushed the button. "Now."

The test car didn't slow down at all. It roared

down the raceway. Under the hood, the carburetor began to glow red with heat.

In the pit, Jack walked over to stand beside Duck. "What's going on?" he asked.

"Megan says we need to know what would happen if the heat sensors didn't shut down the engine," Duck answered. "So she's testing it."

Jack grabbed the radio away from Duck. "Megan," he ordered, "I want you to bring the car in and let one of the drivers take over."

"Too late, Dad," Megan replied over the radio.

The test car continued to blaze down the track at full speed.

"The carb's too hot," Megan reported. "The throttle's stuck wide open."

"You're not a driver, Megan!" Jack shouted into the hand-held radio. "You should be doing advanced research and working on experimental designs! You've got a brilliant mind—you'd just be wasting it behind the wheel of a car!"

Megan glared coldly out the windshield of the test car as it plunged through a loop. When she reached a straightaway, she said, "I guess that means you've decided not to let me race."

A single tear trailed down her cheek.

Jack tried to calm himself down and speak to his daughter in a normal tone of voice. "Megan," he said, "I've staked everything I've got on New Motor

City. On the future. But the real future of Fassler Experimental Technologies is *you*."

Vaaaaaaarrrrrrrrrrrooooooooooooooommmmmm!

Megan's test car let out a deafening roar. Under the hood, orange flames began to shoot out of the carburetor!

"I've always dreamed that some day you'd take over Fastex," Jack said over the radio.

"I've got dreams, too, Dad—" Megan began, but then she noticed the temperature gauge. The needle on the gauge jumped off the red end of the scale. "Duck!" she shouted. "We're going critical!"

Duck grabbed the radio back from Jack. "Get outta there, Megan!" he yelled.

Megan yanked on the wheel, throwing the car into a skid. The test car careened toward the infield.

"How long before it explodes?" Jack asked Duck.

"That's what we're trying to find out," Duck replied.

The test car bounced over the paved infield, its engine engulfed in flame. Megan flipped her Rescue Racer lever.

Shrooop!

The Rescue Racer launched out of the top of the test car. Inside the high-tech escape pod, Megan threw the maneuvering jet lever sideways. Jets fired along the Rescue Racer's side, spinning the small vehicle around in the opposite direction. It hit the infield with a screech of its tires.

The escape pod's tires squealed again as Megan motored it away from the driverless test car as fast as she could.

Kaaaaa-blaaaaaaaaaammmmmmmmmm!

The test car exploded into a bright ball of searing orange and yellow flame. The blast expanded across the infield, reaching toward the escaping Rescue Racer.

But Megan managed to speed to safety.

Jack and Duck watched the ball of flame rise over Big River Raceway. Then they quickly covered their heads as a few smoking chunks of the test car rained down around them, clattering to the ground.

Megan pulled the Rescue Racer to a stop beside the hauler.

Jack stared out at the fiery destruction in the infield, slowly shaking his head.

"There would've been thousands of people in that infield during a race," Duck said softly.

"And thousands more in the grandstands," Jack added.

They glanced at each other.

Fear was written on their faces.

12

The Motorsphere looked even more impressive than usual lit up against the night sky.

Inside, a huge party was going on. Spotlights trailed over the top of the sphere, and on the floor, big tables were set up with food and drink. Giant video projectors threw scenes of Team Fastex cars racing along the high, curving walls. The floor was teeming with drivers, car owners, crew chiefs, and lots and lots of media people.

Two sports announcers stood in front of an enormous Team Fastex logo. "This is the heart of New Motor City," an announcer boomed into his microphone. "The spectacular Motorsphere!"

The announcer paused for applause. "It's media night in the Motorsphere," he continued after the clapping had died down, "and Sports Network

Interglobal Television is bringing it to you live!" He and his partner were wearing matching blazers with the initials SNIT sewn on the pocket.

"Hello, I'm Mike Hauger," the first announcer introduced himself, running a hand through his jet-black hair.

"And I'm Pat Anther," the second announcer said. She had a lot of blond hair and a huge smile.

"And we're here," Mike continued, "to meet the drivers of the supercars of NASCAR's new Unlimited Series!"

Next to the announcers, Stunts, Charger, and Flyer stood in a row, smiling for the cameras, having their pictures taken, and being interviewed. On the other side of the guys from Team Fastex were the members of Team Rexcor, and past them were many more drivers from other teams.

Stunts put on a cap that had the words PILGRIM STATE MOTOR OIL—the name of a sponsor—printed on it. He smiled wide as a camera flashed in his face.

Pat Anther pushed her way next to Charger. "I'm here with Mark 'Charger' McCutchen," she said into the microphone. "Charger, your grandfather was the legendary Mack McCutchen. And your father, Junior McCutchen, also had an outstanding career in racing. You must feel tremendous pressure to live up to that family tradition."

Charger had no idea what to say to that.

Next to him, Stunts switched his Pilgrim State

Motor Oil cap for one that read FLEXOCO GASOLINE. He smiled for another picture.

A different photographer approached Team Rexcor. "Smile, Hondo!" the photographer called.

Hondo looked grim. "I am smiling," he said.

Stunts switched his cap again. This time it read GREAT YEAR TIRES. Once again, he grinned as his picture was taken.

Flashbulbs were going off all over the dome. Zorina posed for the cameras. She had ripped the sleeves off her uniform, and she flexed her muscles as photographers took picture after picture of her.

Charger and Flyer looked dazed as the flashes exploded in their faces. They were wearing caps that read TEAM FASTEX.

Meanwhile, Megan was standing behind the photographers, watching the Team Fastex guys get their pictures taken. She swallowed, and then turned away sadly. She had wanted to be on the team more than she had ever wanted anything, and now she was feeling very left out.

On the other side of Zorina, a photographer aimed his camera at Lyle and Diesel. Lyle put his arm around Diesel's shoulders and grinned.

Diesel glared at Lyle. "No one is touching Diesel Spitz," he hissed. "You get me?"

Lyle quickly pulled his arm away as the photographer took the picture.

• • •

After a while, the media circus temporarily let up a bit, so Stunts and Flyer wandered over to the refreshment table. As they filled their plates, Stunts asked, "Where's your girlfriend tonight, man? She's easy on the eyes—you know what I mean?"

Flyer popped a carrot into his mouth as he shook his head sadly. "She doesn't like racing," he explained.

On the other side of the Motorsphere floor, Mike Hauger was interviewing Jack.

"I believe there's more at stake here than just winning races," Jack said. "At Fastex, we believe that the future depends on learning to control technology, to master the machine. We believe that the future is . . . Unlimited."

Jack nodded as the floor broke out in applause.

But one person wasn't clapping.

Garner Rexton was watching the show from his office, on TV. His hands were clenched into fists on his desk.

"Jack," Garner said, "you don't have a future."

Garner peered at the TV as Duck wandered over to Jack onscreen. The Team Fastex crew chief was gnawing on a chicken leg, which made his words difficult to hear with his mouth full.

But Garner heard them.

And what he heard made his stomach clench with jealousy.

"Jack," Duck said, "there's a call from your wife."

Jack's wife.

Libby.

The only woman Garner Rexton had ever loved.

The woman Jack Fassler had stolen from him.

Libby Fassler's holographic image flickered in front of the desk in Jack's office. Every now and then static shot through the image—it wasn't the best connection. Libby was wearing jungle fatigues and a floppy sun hat. It was the perfect gear for a scientist working in the tropical rain forest, which she was. Libby looked like an older version of Megan, her daughter.

"It's the rainy season here, Jack," Libby said. "This silly holophone you sent me is full of mildew."

Jack was sitting on the edge of his desk. He smiled fondly at his wife.

"You and your gadgets," Libby continued. "Why can't we talk on an ordinary cell phone?"

"Because I like to look at you," Jack replied. "What about the race next week? Will you be able to make it?"

For a moment, the static interrupted the connection and Libby fuzzed out. Jack stood up from the desk.

But the image sharpened slightly so that he could see his wife again. "We're trying to save a rain

forest here, Jack," Libby said. "I can't just pack up and—"

Again, the static made Libby blur.

"Libby," Jack said. "I'm losing you."

The connection faded in, but Libby's words were crackly and hard to hear. "Has she told you she wants to drive?" Libby asked.

"You mean Megan?" Jack said. "Has she talked to you about it?"

"I know my daughter, Jack," Libby said. "She's always loved everything about cars. And if she really wants to race, nothing will stop her." The static broke her image apart momentarily. "You know she's just like you—"

The holographic picture dissolved completely.

"Libby?" Jack asked. He stepped toward the place where the image had hovered. He reached out to touch the stream of static. "Can you hear—"

The picture suddenly snapped into clarity.

But it wasn't Libby. It was a perfectly clear image of Garner Rexton.

Jack jumped backward as though he'd been burned. "Garner!" he exclaimed.

"Yes, Jack," Garner said. "I broke into your call. I hope it wasn't important."

In the hologram, Garner licked his lips. "I think we should talk," he said.

13

*B*ack on the floor of the Motorsphere, the media craziness continued.

Pat Anther slipped through the crowd to stand
next to Flyer. She raised the microphone to her
mouth. "Steve 'Flyer' Sharp, would you like to tell us
what made you decide to leave the Air Force and
become a NASCAR supercar racer?"

Flyer stared at the announcer for a long moment.
Finally, he blinked, and replied, "No, ma'am. I'd
rather not tell you."

Over by the drink table, Zorina filled a paper cup
with purple liquid from a huge punch bowl. On the
side of the cup was printed the word FIZZ, which was
the name of a kind of soda—and a possible sponsor.

Stunts appeared beside Zorina. "*Oye*, Zorina," he
said smoothly. "Why don't you and me go some-

where quiet and explore some long-term investment strategies?"

Zorina sneered at him. "I'm not going anywhere, baby," she said, "until I finish my drink."

Then she hurled the drink into Stunts's face. Purple punch dribbled down his nose.

"There," Zorina said. "Now it's done." She handed the Fizz cup to Stunts and stalked off.

"I get it," Stunts said cheerfully. "She's playing hard to get."

A second later, a guy wearing a yellow blazer with the word FIZZ stitched on the pocket rushed up to Stunts. "Hi," he said. "I'm a vice-president of the Fizz Company." He glanced at the Fizz cup that Zorina had stuck in Stunts's hand. "I see you drink Fizz cola!" the vice-president continued. "Can we talk business, Carlos?"

Stunts stared at the Fizz VP, surprised. But then a big smile crossed Stunts's face. "I'm *always* ready to talk business," he replied.

Near the edge of the crowd, Charger stood beside Megan. Megan was looking down at her feet, lost in thought.

"I don't think it's fair," Charger told Megan, "your dad not letting you drive for Fastex. I mean, after building the cars . . . I think you deserve to drive."

Megan raised her head to meet Charger's

eyes. "Thank you," she said softly. "That means a lot to me."

She was about to say something else, but right then Lyle wandered over, interrupting her.

"Scoring some points with the boss's daughter, McCutchen?" Lyle teased Charger. He slipped between Charger and Megan, and locked eyes with Megan. "How would you like to meet some *real* drivers, Megan?"

Charger slammed his hand down on Lyle's shoulder, and turned him halfway around. "How would you like to get lost?" Charger demanded.

Lyle spun to face his enemy, and knocked Charger's hand off his shoulder. "Trying to stab me in the back again?" Lyle asked with a smirk. "You've already gotten me fired."

With that, Lyle shoved Charger—hard.

Stumbling backward, Charger tried to regain his balance. But he bumped into somebody. Charger whirled around to see that he'd smacked into Diesel Spitz. Diesel was holding an empty plate, and food was all over his feet.

Diesel grabbed Charger by his shirtfront. "Don't be touching the Junker!" he snarled. Then he lifted Charger . . . and hurled him into the air!

Nearby, Stunts was still talking to the Fizz VP. The vice-president leaned over to whisper in Stunts's ear.

"We can pay you a lot more than Team Fastex," the VP said softly.

Crash!

Both Stunts and the Fizz VP turned around quickly to see what had happened behind them.

Diesel had thrown Charger right into the middle of the food table! Charger tried to get up, but Diesel rushed over and grabbed a metal folding chair. The tall Rexcor driver held the chair over his head, ready to smash it down onto Charger.

Flyer was still talking to Pat Anther. When he heard the commotion, he turned to look, and then glanced back at the interviewer. "Excuse me, ma'am," he said.

Diesel let out a bellow of rage as he began to swing the chair down at Charger.

Before the chair could hit, Flyer grabbed Diesel, and flipped him over his shoulder.

Stunts was watching the fight with an amused smile on his face. "Crazy, huh?" he asked the Fizz VP.

"Yo, Stunts!" a female voice yelled.

Stunts turned around to see who'd called his name. Right behind him was Zorina, with her heavily muscled arm pulled back to throw a punch.

"Ay!" Stunts exclaimed. He ducked.

Zorina's punch missed Stunts . . . but hit the Fizz VP right in the nose!

Meanwhile, after Diesel recovered from his flip, he jumped to his feet and charged Flyer like a bull. But before he could reach him, Duck stepped between them. "Break it up!" Duck hollered.

Sploosh!

Someone threw all the purple liquid in the punch bowl right into Duck's face.

Duck angrily wiped his eyes. "Okay!" he demanded. "Who threw that punch?"

Mike Hauger grabbed a cameraman and a microphone and set up a report right in front of the brawl. Behind him, shouts and crashes filled the Motorsphere.

"Is NASCAR's new Unlimited Series fiercely competitive?" Mike asked the camera.

A driver tumbled through the air behind him, yelling. Mike had to sidestep to get out of the way.

With a little grin, Mike answered his own question. "You bet it is," he said.

After Charger managed to clean some of the food off his clothes, he found Lyle by the Motorsphere exit door. Charger shoved Lyle outside.

"You've been asking for a serious butt-kicking," Charger told Lyle. "And I'm going to give it to you."

Lyle held up his hands. "Hey," he said, "we're not fighters. We're *drivers*. Let's settle this our way."

Charger narrowed his eyes. "What do you mean?" he asked.

Zorina had followed them out the exit door. She rubbed her knuckles where they were red and sore from punching the Fizz VP.

"He means a *race*, baby," Zorina answered for Lyle.

Back up in Jack's office, he was still talking to the hologram of Garner.

"I don't expect favors because we used to be partners," Jack said. "But you know how much New Motor City will be worth once Unlimited Series racing becomes a success—"

The hologram of Garner raised a hand sharply, silencing Jack. "If you don't make the loan payment due at the end of this month," he said, "I'll have to foreclose."

Jack's hands curled into fists. "You can't take New Motor City away from me!" he exclaimed.

Garner shrugged. "You borrowed millions from EnormaBanc to build it," he replied. "Now that I own EnormaBanc—"

"You have to give me more time!" Jack broke in.

"It's nothing personal, Jack," Garner said. "It's business."

Then the hologram of Garner Rexton dissolved, leaving Jack Fassler alone with his anger.

And a really big problem.

14

*B*RRRRRMMMMM!

In the New Motor City parking lot, Flyer started his Jeep. He flicked on the headlights and started toward the lot's exit.

Before he had traveled more than a few feet, however, he stopped abruptly.

Standing in the beam of his headlights was Megan Fassler, blocking Flyer's path. Her arms were crossed over her chest.

As soon as she saw that Flyer had stopped, Megan hurried over to the driver-side window. "Charger is going to race Lyle Owens, isn't he?" she demanded.

Flyer closed his eyes for a moment. "It's a guy thing, Megan—"

"It's a *dumb* thing," Megan broke in. "And I'm not going to let him do it."

"Megan," Flyer said, "I've got to go—"

"Okay," Megan replied. "I guess I won't tell my father about this race, if that's what you're worried about. After all, I haven't told him anything about your odd little attacks. . . ." She let her voice trail off.

Flyer got her meaning loud and clear. He sat quietly for a moment, staring at her. Finally, he heaved a big sigh.

"Since Charger's car is wrecked," Flyer explained, "they're going to race in their escape pods—their Rescue Racers. At the diner."

"Thank you, Flyer," Megan said. "That's exactly what I wanted to know."

The diner's big neon sign blinked and buzzed in the darkness.

Vrrrmmmm! Vrrrmmmm!

On the road in front of the diner, two Rescue Racers were lined up side by side, revving their engines. Charger was in his souped-up escape pod, and Lyle was in a similar Team Rexcor version. Stunts was standing nearby, amid the small crowd who had come out of the diner to watch the race.

In front of the two Rescue Racers, Zorina stood in the middle of the road, her long, dark hair fluttering

in the breeze. She held a white handkerchief in her hand.

"When I drop this handkerchief," Zorina yelled, "take off!"

Slowly, Zorina raised the hand that held the white flag as high as she could reach.

The handkerchief fluttered in the wind. . . .

Back in the Motorsphere parking lot, Megan hurried to her car. She opened the door—

"Megan!" she heard.

Turning around, Megan saw her father striding toward her. Jack caught up to his daughter quickly.

"I'm kind of in a hurry, Dad," Megan told him.

Jack ignored her. "How much do you want to drive, Megan?" he asked.

Megan's heart lurched. She stared at her father's face to make sure he wasn't joking.

With a nod, Jack continued. "Do you want to drive enough to stake everything on one race?" he asked. "One chance to make a dream come true?"

"Are you saying I can drive in the first race?" Megan asked.

Jack took a deep breath. "I'm going to give you a chance to prove yourself," he replied.

A little smile played at the corners of Megan's lips. The smile was quickly replaced by a look of fierce determination. Her father was giving her a chal-

lenge. And Megan Fassler *never* turned down a challenge.

"A chance is all I need," Megan said.

The handkerchief held high in Zorina's hand whipped in the breeze.

Inside Charger's Rescue Racer, he gripped the steering wheel firmly and revved his engine. *Vrrrmmmm!*

In his own escape vehicle, Owens was also focused on the road ahead of him. He revved his motor, too.

Zorina let go of the handkerchief.

Charger slammed his gas pedal to the floor.

The two Rescue Racers sprang ahead, one on either side of Zorina.

The roar of their racers wasn't nearly as loud as the Unlimited Series cars, but was loud enough to rattle the windows of the diner.

Gravel shot out from behind the racers' tires as they surged down the road.

Zorina grabbed her handkerchief out of the air before it hit the ground. She waved it wildly.

"Go Rexcor!" she screamed.

Charger and Lyle blasted into the dark woods. Their headlights splashed a flickering white glow over the trees as the two Rescue Racers streamed down the winding forest roads.

Neither driver was gaining much of a lead. Neck and neck they crested a hill so fast that their vehicles soared off the road for a second.

Their tires shrieked as they landed again. The two drivers whizzed into the thick darkness, leaving the diner far behind.

On a short straightaway, Lyle hauled on his steering wheel—veering right at Charger's Rescue Racer.

"You owe me, McCutchen!" Lyle hollered. "And I'm *collecting*!"

With a sickening crunch of metal, Lyle banged into the side of Charger's racer.

Charger narrowed his eyes. He had a few tricks up his sleeve, too. It was time to teach Lyle Owens a lesson.

The Rescue Racers pulled apart again, but not for long. This time, it was Charger who yanked hard on his wheel, steering his racer toward Lyle's.

But at the same time, Charger pressed his brakes.

Instead of slamming into the side of Lyle's racer, Charger's vehicle walloped the edge of Lyle's rear bumper.

Klaannngg!

The force of the collision spun Lyle's Rescue Racer, whipping it out of control.

Lyle's vehicle thrashed off the road, flinging into a shallow ditch.

Sploosh!

The ditch was filled with water.

"Charge!" Charger yelled, his voice filled with excitement.

Now there was nothing but open road through the trees ahead of him, and Charger blasted down it without wasting another moment.

Down in the ditch, Lyle swore as he jammed his Rescue Racer into low gear.

Grrriiinnndd! A horrible rasping sound filled the woods.

The grinding gears sounded terrible, but the low gear worked, giving Lyle the traction he needed. Slowly, Lyle managed to drive the escape pod back up onto the road.

And then Lyle was off again after Charger.

He had a lot of catching up to do.

15

*U*p the road through the forest was a deep, dark quarry.

The quarry had steep, stone walls a hundred feet high, ripped clean years ago by miners. Thick trees and plants covered the tops of the walls, and far below, a wide lake shimmered in the moonlight. A few leftover flat boulders stuck out from the lake's calm surface.

The only sounds were frogs singing and the buzz of insects, until—

Rrmm! Rrmm!

The two Rescue Racers could be heard far in the distance.

A dirt road led to the quarry, forking off from the main road. At that fork, in front of the dirt road, a big, wooden warning barrier blocked off the road. On the barrier was a sign that read ROAD ENDS.

Next to the sign stood Diesel Spitz and Hondo Hines.

Hondo watched as Diesel grabbed the whole wooden barrier and struggled to lift it. Diesel carried the barrier over to the main road and put it down in the middle.

"You might be helping me," Diesel complained to Hondo. "Maybe."

"Hey," Hondo replied, "I came up with this idea. I've done my part."

Diesel fixed the barrier so that it looked like it had been there a long time, blocking the main road. "This Charger McCutchen will be taking the wrong road, right?" Diesel said. "And then he is junk!"

Rrmmmm! Rrmmmm!

The sound of the approaching Rescue Racers grew louder.

"They're coming," Hondo said. "Let's get out of here."

The two members of Team Rexcor hurried to hide in the bushes.

Headlights flashed in the distance as the Rescue Racers drove closer. Then Charger swooped around a turn and barreled down the road.

Lyle wasn't too far behind—he had nearly caught up to Charger.

Charger sped up on the straightaway. He didn't

even pause as he whipped down the fork that led to the quarry.

A second later, Lyle zoomed down the same straightaway.

Crash!

Lyle smashed right through the barrier and continued down the main road. He smiled as he drove. "Good-bye, country boy," he said. The Collector knew this race was his, and Charger would finally get what he deserved.

The cliff of the quarry glistened in the glare of Charger's headlights.

It took another few seconds for Charger to notice that the road suddenly ended in front of his vehicle. "Whoa!" he yelled as he stomped on the brakes.

The Rescue Racer couldn't stop immediately on the dirt road. It slid over the gravel, slipping toward the edge of the quarry's cliff.

Charger yanked desperately on the steering wheel, pumping the brake, but it was no use. The escape pod kept skidding toward the edge.

Then it caught on a ridge of rock, and flipped over, tumbling end over end toward the cliff.

A thick tree jutted up in Charger's whirling view. The Rescue Racer slammed into the trunk, knocking the tree to the ground.

With a bone-jarring jerk, Charger stopped.

He quickly peeked out his windshield. The tree had fallen over, and half of it was hanging over the

edge of the cliff. His Rescue Racer was caught in the branches, dangling over the lake far, far below. Charger had to get out—now!

Charger scrambled to unbuckle his safety harness. The tree gave a sickening crack. The branches were giving way!

Snaaa-apppp!

The Rescue Racer shifted downward as a branch below broke off.

A moment later, the last supporting branch snapped, and the racer tumbled down to the water below.

The Rescue Racer landed upside down on one of the boulders in the lake. The vehicle warped and flattened from the impact.

Then, slowly, it began to slide off the flat, sloping rock.

The racer's metal body scraped against the boulder as it lazily slid toward the water. After a long, drawn-out glide over the rock, the Rescue Racer finally splashed into the lake.

The smashed cockpit was under the surface. Only one wheel could be seen poking out of the water.

Silence fell over the quarry.

After a few moments, the frogs began to sing again, and the insects returned to buzzing.

The only movement from the Rescue Racer was from the single tire sticking out of the lake.

It turned slowly . . . but that was only from the wind.

16

Less than ten minutes later, Megan pulled up beside the edge of the quarry in her little red sports car. Flyer and Stunts arrived in Flyer's Jeep and parked next to her.

Megan quickly hopped out of the car and walked carefully to the cliff. She peered down. What she saw made her stomach drop. "There's Charger's Rescue Racer!" she called. "In the water!"

Stunts and Flyer ran up beside her.

"Charger!" Megan shouted desperately. "Charger!"

"You don't have to yell," Charger said.

Megan, Flyer, and Stunts looked around. They had heard Charger clearly, but they couldn't see him anywhere. "Where are you?" Megan called.

"Down here," Charger said.

The three teammates looked down the cliff's sheer face. Charger was dangling from the toppled tree, clinging to the branches. "About time you got here," Charger said.

Flyer and Stunts rushed over to help Charger out of the tree. They grabbed his hands and pulled him up to the safety of the ledge.

"How did you get out of the Rescue Racer?" Megan asked.

"I used the door," Charger replied. "Is there another way out?"

With that, Charger walked past his teammates and headed for the Jeep.

Stunts glanced at Megan. "He's got a point there," he said. Then he turned, too, and followed Charger to the Jeep. Flyer hurried after them.

Megan closed her eyes and let out a long sigh.

Later that night, Lyle, Zorina, Hondo, and Diesel were having a celebration in the diner. A pitcher of Fizz cola was on the table, and everybody had a glass.

"A toast," Lyle said, holding up his glass. "To Team Rexcor's first victory!"

"One driver down," Hondo said. He clinked his glass with Zorina's. "And three to go."

Suddenly, Megan appeared beside the table. "Is this a private toast," she asked, "or can anyone join in?"

Lyle laughed and shifted in his chair. "I can squeeze you in beside me," he said.

Megan grabbed the pitcher of Fizz off the table. She held it up as though she was proposing a toast. "To a real jerk," she announced.

Then she splashed the entire pitcher over Lyle's head.

Diesel and Zorina cracked up as Lyle jumped to his feet, his face red with anger. But Megan had already dropped the pitcher and stormed away.

The next day, all of Team Rexcor gathered around Spex in the Rexcor garage. On the video screen built into Spex's chest, Garner Rexton stared out at his team.

"This isn't just a race," Garner said. "It's a war. Team Fastex is your enemy. They must not be allowed to win the first Unlimited Series race."

All the drivers listened solemnly to their boss.

After a long pause, Garner continued speaking. "I will give each of you a bonus of one million dollars," he said, "if Team Fastex loses."

A low murmur rippled through the garage. Zorina sat up straight, and Hondo and Diesel glanced at each other, sharing an excited look.

Garner stared out of Spex's chest directly at Lyle. "And Mr. Owens is going to make it easier for you," he said, "by making sure that one Team Fastex

driver will never finish the race. Isn't that right, Mr. Owens?"

"Yes, sir," Lyle replied. "That's the plan."

Flyer was asleep in his apartment bedroom, having an awful nightmare.

In the dream, Flyer was cruising in an Air Force jet fighter over the desert. A missile exploded directly beside his fighter. A thin spiderweb crack appeared on Flyer's windshield. His jet spun in the air, out of control.

Flyer struggled with the controls as the jet tumbled out of the sky. He was wearing an Air Force uniform, a flight helmet, and night-vision goggles.

"I'm hit!" Flyer yelled. "Mayday! Mayday!"

His only hope was to get back to the base for a crash landing. Luckily, the military complex wasn't too far away.

Flyer swooped over a cluster of buildings disguised by desert camouflage. A strange, sinister red cloud billowed up from the main building, which had been heavily damaged in the battle. Oddly, the cloud didn't float in the air like smoke—it looked more like blood mixing with water.

Trying desperately to keep his jet's nose up, Flyer skimmed over the military complex. Black smoke poured out of one of his wings.

Suddenly, the strange, frightening red mist splat-

tered all across Flyer's windshield. It dripped through the crack in the glass—

Flyer woke up falling out of bed.

Whaam!

He rubbed his shoulder where he'd landed on it. "Just a bad dream," he whispered to himself. "It was just a dream."

But Flyer couldn't get rid of a terrible fear stuck in his chest. He tried to breathe deeply, but it was difficult.

"Something bad's going to happen . . ." Flyer gasped.

His hand was shaking.

Flyer made a fist, forcing the shaking to stop.

17

*I*t was a beautiful, sunny day at Big
River Raceway.

Flyer took advantage of the sunshine and went for
a jog in the infield.

Vvvrrrrrrooooooooommmmmmmmmmm!

On the track, Charger whipped past Flyer in his
Unlimited Series car. He concentrated on taking an
upcoming turn at a speed he'd never managed
before.

Jack, Megan, and Duck stood in the pits, watching
Charger drive. As Charger passed the pit wall,
Megan checked out a hand-held computer.

"Those adjustments I made on the carburetor are
keeping it from overheating," she reported.

Jack nodded. "Races are won and lost in the
garage," he said solemnly.

Megan glanced at him. "Nice try, Dad," she snapped. "But I still want to drive."

With those words, Megan stuck the portable computer into her father's hands and stormed away.

Jack and Duck watched her as she left. "Driving is hard, loud, hot, dirty work," Jack said. "One race, and she'll be ready to quit."

Duck cleared his throat. "You don't know your daughter very well, do you?" he said.

"What do you mean?" Jack asked, glancing at Duck.

"When she makes up her mind," Duck replied, "Megan's a regular spitfire."

Meanwhile, Stunts stood outside the Fastex headquarters, waiting impatiently.

In a few moments, a long, black limo pulled up in front of him. On the side of the limousine was a small, tasteful Fizz Cola logo.

The rear window of the limo slid down, revealing the Fizz vice-president.

Stunts leaned into the window. "So," he said, "let's get right to the point. Were you serious about paying me more than Team Fastex to drive for you?"

The Fizz VP nodded. "It's not just that we can pay you more to drive, Carlos," he said. "As a spokesman for Fizz Cola, you'd be doing commercials seen all over the world."

Now that was what Stunts liked to hear. Money . . . *and* fame. It was an offer that he'd be stupid to pass up. Still, he didn't want to look *too* eager.

"I can't leave Team Fastex until after this race, anyway," Stunts told the VP. "I'll have to let you know then."

"You think about it," the Fizz VP said. Then the VP pressed a button inside the limo and the window began to rise.

Stunts stepped back, and watched as the limousine drove away.

It *was* a great offer. Megabucks, *plus* his face on every TV screen all over the world.

So then why did Stunts feel so uncomfortable when he thought about leaving Team Fastex?

The three-quarter moon illuminated the Motorsphere with silvery light. The same glow glistened on the empty parking lot and the Team Fastex hauler.

At that time of night, the hauler was supposed to be empty, too.

Which was why Spex and Lyle had chosen that time to break in.

Spex and Lyle stood next to Charger's Unlimited Series car in the dark. Spex held up a small computer chip. "This new chip will make certain that the engine overheats," Spex explained in his robotic

voice. "It also keeps the engine from shutting down."

Lyle had been keeping his distance from the strange Rexcor crew chief, but when Spex opened the hood of Charger's car, he pushed it down again. "Not McCutchen's car," Lyle said. "I want to take him out personally . . . during the race."

Spex withdrew and Lyle clicked Charger's hood shut. Then Lyle walked over to one of the other cars in the hauler. "Mr. Rexton said it didn't matter which car we sabotaged," he told Spex. "Put the chip in this one, okay?"

One of Spex's fingers suddenly erupted with the blue flame of a blowtorch. Lyle decided to take that as a "yes."

Lyle popped the hood on the car in front of him, and watched as Spex got to work. The light of the blowtorch glowed eerily in Spex's mechanical eyes.

While he was waiting for Spex to finish installing the chip, Lyle checked to see whose car they were "fixing."

A name on the door read FLYER.

18

*R*ace day had finally arrived.

The giant Motorsphere gleamed in the sunlight. The parking lot was filled to capacity with cars, trucks, and camper vans. Above the Motorsphere, a huge blimp floated lazily. The blimp was in the shape of a can of soda with fins, and it had the word FIZZ written on it in enormous letters.

The bustling crowd slowly filed into the stands of Big River Raceway. They were busy checking out the new track, marveling at the gigantic dome, and buying refreshments and souvenirs.

The pits were crazy crowded, too. Pit road was lined with Unlimited Series cars from all the teams. Crews worked frantically on the cars, getting them ready for the big race. Duck and Megan were right in the middle, taking care of last minute adjustments to the Team Fastex cars. Nearby, Hondo and Lyle watched Spex fixing up their racers.

Inside the Team Fastex hauler, it was extremely quiet compared to the roar of the crowd outside. Charger zipped up his snappy uniform. Next to him, Flyer was sitting on a chair, mentally preparing himself for the race. He raised one hand and held it in front of his face. Steady.

Over the infield, a group of parachutists jumped out of an airplane. They trailed colored smoke on the way down, crossing the streams to make a giant X in the air. The crowd bellowed its approval with applause and cheers.

Jack was too busy to appreciate the parachute show. He stood in pit road with his arms crossed, watching two NASCAR technicians carefully. The technicians had a big metal template, which they held up to each Unlimited Series car—making sure that the racers were within the specifications set by the Division.

Up in the broadcast booth, the announcers began their coverage of the race. "Welcome to Sports Network Interglobal Television's coverage of the Motorsphere 500!" one announcer boomed through the loudspeaker. "It's the first race in NASCAR's new Unlimited Series!"

The crowd went berserk with applause.

"Hi, I'm Mike Hauger," the first announcer continued.

"And I'm Pat Anther," the second one said. Both the announcers were wearing their blazers with the SNIT logo printed on the pocket.

"We're about to get things underway," Mike said, "here at Big River Raceway in New Motor City!"

The announcers peered out the big window of their broadcast booth down at the track far below. The stands were jam-packed with cheering fans, and the infield was covered with RVs and more fans. The pit area on the side of the track was filled with IMPs, with each team's hauler behind their IMP. A double line of Unlimited Division cars waited on pit road for the signal.

The track PA system squawked to life.

"Drivers," a voice boomed over the raceway, echoing against the stands.

"Start your engines!"

19

All *the drivers hit their starter* buttons. The roar of all the engines booming into life at once shook the stands.

The pace car led the Unlimited Series racers through the first lap. The cars began to accelerate.

As the line of vehicles passed where Jack and Duck were standing by the pit wall, Jack turned to his crew chief.

"If we don't win this race, Duck," Jack said softly, "I could lose Fastex."

Duck blinked at him, too surprised to reply.

The line of cars came around a turn and headed into a straightaway. That's when the pace car peeled off and zoomed down pit road.

All eyes in the crowd were fixed on the blank video screen hanging above the starting line.

Suddenly, a waving green flag appeared on the screen.

Vvvvvrrrrrrrrrrrroooooooooooommmmmmmm!

The crowd hollered its approval as the cars exploded off down the track.

Within minutes, the lines of racers were sizzling down the track so fast they were nothing but brightly colored blurs.

On top of the Team Fastex hauler, Miles McCutchen had helped his mother climb up onto the twin seats of the hauler's observation tower.

"We'll be able to see better from up here, Mom," Miles said.

Miles found a group of levers sticking out from under the seats. He grabbed one and threw it.

Miles and his mother both cried out in surprise as the seats they were sitting on suddenly shot into the sky. The seats were on a telescoping hydraulic system that could extend far up like a radio antenna.

Far up above the hauler, Miles held on to the seat as he checked out his awesome view of all of Big River Raceway.

"Way cool!" Miles exclaimed.

The race went hot and heavy from the start.

Stunts was in the lead, with Zorina close behind. The Motorsphere loomed up ahead, and Stunts whizzed into the darkness of the entrance tunnel.

He gushed out into the dome's vast interior, zooming across the straightaway that led across the sphere's floor.

Zorina accelerated, pulling up close to Stunts's car.

When they had reached the far side of the Motorsphere, Zorina and Stunts were nearly neck and neck. As they glided up the curved wall of the dome, Zorina threw a lever on her instrument panel.

"A million dollars, baby!" Zorina shouted. If she took Stunts out, that was exactly how much money she would earn. Of course, Zorina would have been happy to take out Stunts for free—but the money was a nice bonus.

Whoooooooooshhh!

Maneuvering jets fired along the side of Zorina's car, pushing her racer into Stunts.

Both cars spun out.

Stunts slammed a control jet lever in his racer. His car skidded along the curved wall, but his firing jets kept him speeding straight ahead.

Zorina, on the other hand, slid up the dome sideways. She fought with the wheel, trying to regain control . . .

A few seconds later, Stunts's car spurted out the exit tunnel of the Motorsphere.

Blaaaaaaaam!

Stunts cringed at the violent explosion behind him, and he smiled as he roared down the track.

After a long pause, Zorina's Rescue Racer puttered out of the exit tunnel. Strips of metal were hanging off her escape pod, and clouds of dark smoke billowed around her. The inside of the Rescue Racer was filled with impact foam, which expanded during a crash to protect the driver.

There was no way she could compete in the Rescue Racer. A disgusted look crossed Zorina's face, and she wiped the sticky foam off her.

"So long, million bucks," she said angrily. "Baby."

Above the starting line, the video screen changed to show a yellow flag.

Mike Hauger leaned forward in the broadcast booth. "With only twenty laps to go," he announced, "we've got a caution flag for debris on the track."

Cars all along the track slowed down for the caution flag.

Except for Flyer.

Megan had slowed down with everyone else, and she was very surprised when Flyer blasted past her on the track. "What are you doing, Flyer?" she shouted.

In the pits, Duck was sitting on the IMP's mechanic's seat, which gave him a good view of the track. He picked up his radio and connected to Flyer. "Flyer!" he yelled. "You can't pass during a yellow flag!"

Inside Flyer's racer, something was terribly wrong. Flyer peered at his gauges in confusion. "It's

stuck at full throttle!" he shouted back to Duck over the radio link. "I'm overheating!"

Jack climbed up on top of the IMP to stand next to Duck. He had his own radio in his hand. "Flyer!" Jack warned. "You can't slow down—or stop! The engine will blow up if you do!"

Flyer nodded, trying to keep concentrating on driving while everyone else around him was going slowly. "Can I run full out until I'm out of fuel?" he asked.

Megan joined the conversation over her car's radio link. "No," she answered. "The heat will reach critical, Flyer. The car will explode before the fuel's gone!"

With a deep breath, Megan continued. "The explosion could kill hundreds of people," she said.

High above the raceway, Garner Rexton was watching from his luxury booth near the broadcast station. He peered down at the track through his high-tech binoculars, watching Flyer buzzing down the track faster than everyone else.

He smiled.

Everything was going according to plan.

Soon the destruction of everything Jack Fassler had worked so hard to build would be complete.

20

*F*lyer's car sizzled down the track.
He was kept very busy weaving between the slower-moving racers, who were obeying the yellow caution flag—who *could* obey the yellow flag.

The radio squawked, and Jack's voice filled Flyer's cockpit. "Flyer," Jack said. "Sharp. I . . . I won't order you to sacrifice your life, but . . . if that car explodes here in New Motor City . . ."

"Sir," was all Flyer said. He understood what Jack meant.

For a long moment, Flyer just focused on driving. Then he gripped the steering wheel tightly. He'd made a decision.

"Mr. Fassler," he said into the radio, "I'm taking it to the river."

Then Flyer hauled on his steering wheel, veering off the track.

"Dad!" Megan called over the radio link. "I'm going with him!"

Without waiting for a reply, Megan yanked on her wheel, following Flyer.

Flyer's path took him right in front of Diesel "Junker" Spitz's car. Diesel glared at Flyer, and then sped up, ignoring the caution.

"I will junk you!" Diesel hollered. He threw a lever on his control shift.

A grappling hook launched out of the front of Diesel's car and flew threw the air, trailing a long cable.

Claaaaangggg!

The hook caught the back bumper of Flyer's car.

At the same time, Flyer pressed his jump lever.

Wings slid out of the sides of Flyer's racer and his turbojet booster erupted with flame. Flyer's car soared into the air.

The line between his car and Diesel's pulled taut. "Arrghh!" Diesel shouted as his racer jerked off the ground.

Flyer sailed over the wall around Big River Raceway, pulling Diesel along with him.

"Let go!" Diesel shouted.

On the other side of the wall, Flyer barely cleared a giant garbage truck that was waiting to haul away

all the trash from the crowd. He landed safely in front of it.

But Diesel didn't. His racer plopped right into the truck's open top—with the rest of the garbage.

"Oh!" Diesel yelled. "Oh, it smells!"

The grappling hook's line snapped, freeing Flyer as his wings pulled in again and his rockets sputtered out. Flyer roared away.

Megan flew her own car over a different part of the wall. Her landing was perfect, and she quickly raced after Flyer's out-of-control car.

Up in the broadcast booth, Mike Hauger and Pat Anther were announcing the race with great excitement.

"Two cars from Team Fastex have left the race track!" Mike called.

"Mike," Pat said in a worried voice, "we're getting reports that one of the cars is about to explode . . ."

Nobody knew the danger better than Megan herself did—she had designed the cars, after all. She contacted Flyer by radio. "You go critical in five minutes, Flyer," she warned him.

Flyer took a deep breath and grabbed the steering wheel so tightly he thought he might crush it. But his voice was calm when he replied.

"Understood," Flyer said.

The two members of Team Fastex barreled away from Big River Raceway, heading toward the tall

towers of downtown New Motor City ahead. They would have to go straight through the city in order to reach the river in time.

A police helicopter swooped in from above, following them.

Under the hood of Flyer's car, the engine was beginning to glow red.

21

Flyer and Megan careened through the streets of New Motor City, whipping down the streets between tall glass and steel sky-scrapers.

They roared around a corner, skidding as they took a heart-stoppingly sharp turn onto a street.

Crrrrrraaaaaaaashhh!

Sploooooooosh!

Before she regained control of her skid, Megan's car whacked into a fire hydrant, sending it flying. Water spewed into the air.

Megan didn't slow down for a second. "Send the bill to Fastex!" she shouted.

The police helicopter buzzed ahead of the drivers, hovering over a busy intersection filled with traffic.

"Clear the road!" the police loudspeaker squawked. "Now!"

People rushed to get out of the way as Megan and Flyer roared through the intersection.

"It's too crowded here, Flyer!" Megan shouted into the radio. "And you can't stop, or you'll explode! Follow me!"

She hurtled straight into a multilevel parking garage, smashing through a yellow wooden barrier.

After she had passed, a ticket popped out of the automatic dispenser. "Please take your ticket," a recorded voice said.

Flyer plunged into the garage after Megan. He was going so fast that the ticket whipped out of the dispenser.

"Thank you," the recorded voice said.

On the far end of the garage, Megan headed right for a concrete wall. She closed her eyes.

Crrrrrruunnnnnnchhhhhh!

Megan smashed right through the concrete wall and landed on the street on the other side. She roared away down the street, with Flyer hot on her bumper.

The two drivers spotted the entrance ramp to the freeway and bolted toward it. They zipped past a sign that pointed out the direction to Riverfront Park.

Flyer and Megan blasted down the freeway, darting around the cars in front of them.

100

But up ahead were a bus and a truck, driving slowly down the freeway side by side. They were blocking the way!

Megan hit her brakes before she hit the bus, but Flyer couldn't stop.

He threw his jump lever.

"Wild blue yonder time!" he shouted as his wings slid out and his rockets erupted.

Flyer soared over the truck, and landed in front of it. With a screech of his tires, he raced on down the freeway.

Megan swerved onto the shoulder and went around the bus.

Back in the pits of Big River Raceway, Jack and Duck checked up on Megan and Flyer on a hand-held computer.

"They're out of time, Jack!" Duck said.

Jack put his hand on his heart. An expression of pure pain crossed his face.

"Megan," he said softly.

Riverfront Park was a quiet, calm garden alongside the river. Tall trees shaded pretty walkways and benches, and beautiful flowers grew in well-tended beds surrounded by grass.

Caa-raaaaaaash!

Flyer smashed through the wooden fence around the park and roared across the grass. His tires tore up the lawn, spouting dirt out behind him.

A sign that read PLEASE KEEP OFF THE GRASS popped up in front of his car.

Flyer crushed it beneath his wheels.

Under the hood, bright red flames began to lick out of the engine.

"It's going critical!" Flyer yelled.

Megan gushed into the park through the hole Flyer had blasted in the fence. "You've gotta get out, Flyer!" she shouted. "Now!"

Flyer's car headed directly for the river. He threw a lever.

The Rescue Racer exploded out of Flyer's car with him inside.

The car sailed over a cliff, plummeting down into the river far below.

Flyer's Rescue Racer fell out of the air, and skidded on a concrete path that bordered the cliff. It slid toward the edge.

Reacting instantly, Megan flicked a lever.

Twwaaaaap!

Her grappling hook shot out the front of her car.

Cllaaaaaaaanngggg!

The hook sailed through the air and hit Flyer's Rescue Racer, catching it.

Perfect shot.

Megan stomped on her brake pedal. As her wheels locked, the car spun out on the grass. A hook-shaped emergency anchor flopped out the back of the car and thudded into the ground.

The Rescue Racer slid off the edge of the cliff. It fell out of sight, trailing the grappling hook line.

The line snapped taut as it pulled Flyer's escape pod to a halt. The sudden stop was so rough that the grappling hook bent the metal panel it had caught on the racer. The panel tore partly loose.

Below Flyer, his car hit the water.

Kaaaaaaaa-blaaaaaaaaaaammmmmmmmmm!

An enormous ball of flames rose up from the exploding car. The fireball spread into the sky. Flyer covered his face so that the intense heat wouldn't scorch his eyes.

Up on top of the cliff, Megan's car had come to a stop—right at the edge. She ran to look down at the river.

Megan felt an incredible sense of relief as she saw the Rescue Racer dangling from the grappling hook, but that lasted only a second.

The Rescue Racer was swinging on the line.

Baaaaaaaaashhhh!

It smacked right into the cliff wall.

The panel that had torn partly free before now started to pull off the Rescue Racer with a screech of metal.

"It's coming loose!" Flyer screamed. He unlocked his safety harness and scrambled out of the Rescue Racer, climbing up on it.

And that was when the metal panel that the grappling hook was attached to gave out.

22

*T*he *Rescue Racer fell.*

Flyer leaped for the end of the grappling hook. He caught it.

As soon as Megan was sure that Flyer had a good grip on the hook, she ran back to her car. She leaned inside.

"Dad!" she shouted over the radio. "It's okay. We're all right."

Then she hurried back to the cliff to help Flyer climb up.

When Flyer was safely up on the ledge, Megan breathed a deep sigh of relief. She didn't think she'd ever felt so exhausted in her life.

Flyer turned to look at her and grinned.

"Piece of cake," he said.

• • •

A big smile covered Jack Fassler's face as he lowered his hand-held radio. He looked at Duck. "They're all right," he said. "They're safe."

Duck grinned, but his expression changed as he noticed someone over Jack's shoulder. "Better tell your wife," he said.

Confused, Jack turned around. Libby Fassler was striding toward him.

"Libby!" Jack cried. "You made it!" He rushed toward her and grabbed her for a big hug.

Garner Rexton watched the happy reunion through his binoculars from his luxury suite. His hands trembled as he watched Jack and Libby kiss.

Finally, he couldn't take it anymore and he lowered the binoculars. An expression of misery made his face look sunken and old.

"Libby . . ." Garner whispered.

He buried his face in his hands.

Garner had never felt more pitiful and lonely.

"There's good news for Team Fastex," Mike Hauger announced in the broadcast booth. "The two drivers who left the race are safe!"

All around the stadium, fans rose to their feet, applauding and cheering.

On the track, Charger wasn't paying any attention to the commotion in the stands. He was too focused on catching up to Lyle and Hondo, who were now in the lead.

After taking the lead early in the race, Stunts had fallen back. He was now side by side with Charger.

Together, Stunts and Charger zoomed past the last car that held a position between them and the Team Rexcor drivers. They leaned into a sharp turn, and then leveled out for a long straightaway.

Jack, Libby, and Duck had climbed up on top of the IMP for a better view. Jack followed his team's efforts through powerful binoculars.

"They're challenging for the lead, Duck!" Jack exclaimed.

Charger's car closed in on the Team Rexcor drivers. Charger concentrated on the track's terrain, knowing from experience how to pick up the most speed.

But it wasn't enough. He would need some help.

Charger flicked a lever.

Whoooooooooshhhh!

"Let's get charged!" Charger hollered as his rocket boosters belched fire. His car sprinted forward, closing the distance between himself and Lyle and Hondo with incredible velocity.

23

Charger *began to ease up past* Lyle, between the two Team Rexcor racers.

Lyle couldn't let that happen. "It's collection time, country boy," he said. Then he threw a lever on his gearshift. The rockets on one side of Lyle's car came to life.

Wham!

Lyle's car smashed into Charger's, knocking it sideways.

Wham!

Charger's car whacked into Hondo's.

Hondo was jolted by the impact, but the jolt gave him an idea. "Hey!" he shouted through his radio to Lyle. "Let's play tennis with him!"

Hauling on his steering wheel, Hondo swerved back toward Charger.

Wham!

Now it was Lyle's turn to swerve.

Wham!

Charger's car bounced between the Team Rexcor vehicles. He fought with the steering while trying to keep his car steady.

Then Charger flipped a lever. "My serve, Collector!" he shouted.

The maneuvering jets alongside Charger's car fired, and he slammed hard into Lyle's car.

Lyle threw his jump lever. "Catch this lob, Charger!" he called.

The side rockets of Lyle's car blasted, launching his car into the air.

The car tilted and started to come down again— on top of Charger's car!

For a second, Charger was stunned by the crash above him. His windshield cracked from the weight of the racer landing on top of his car.

Behind them, Stunts's eyes grew wide. "Hey!" he shouted. "Get off him!"

It was Stunts's turn to flip a lever. The same rockets he'd used to avoid hitting Miles a few days ago now erupted—pushing his car up on two wheels.

Stunts slammed his gas pedal down, and rushed toward the cars ahead of him. As he neared, still on two wheels, he aimed his car just right . . .

The top of Stunts's car caught the rear bumper of

109

Lyle's racer on top of Charger's car. Lyle began spinning like a top.

Dizziness threatened to overwhelm Lyle as his car rotated. "What's going on?" he yelled.

Then the front end of Lyle's spinning car hit Hondo's windshield.

"Lyle!" Hondo screamed. The front tire of Lyle's car was sticking through the glass.

Lyle's car couldn't spin on top of Charger forever. The wind caught it, and Lyle slid off the back of Charger's car.

The impact of Lyle's car hitting the track knocked Stunts's racer over.

On the other side of Charger, Hondo spun out—he couldn't see the track anymore with his windshield shattered.

Lyle's car rolled over and filled with impact foam. "Hey!" Lyle shouted.

Stunts's racer flipped end over end down the track before coming to a stop against the wire fence along the edge of the raceway.

Hondo skidded into the low infield wall.

Wham!

His cockpit filled with impact foam, too, as his car bumped up on the top of the wall, jamming there.

Lyle's car stopped rolling, landing right side up.

Charger raced on ahead.

Stunts climbed out of his car and managed to

untangle himself from the shredded wire fence. A female gasp made him turn around.

Behind the fence, three pretty girls were staring at Stunts's horribly battered car. They all looked very worried.

Stunts smiled and waved to the girls. "Hey, *chicas,*" he said. "Wanna go for a ride?"

24

Charger *motored down the Big River Raceway track*, gliding around a curve.

Up in the broadcast booth, Mike Hauger leaned over his microphone in excitement. "Charger McCutchen has taken the lead coming into the final stretch!" he announced breathlessly. "Nothing can stop him now!"

Ahead of Charger, he could see the video screen above the finish line. He was in the home stretch—with nobody else around.

"Go Charger!" Miles and Mrs. McCutchen hollered from the observation tower.

Under Charger's hood, though, his engine was starting to glow red.

As Charger cruised toward victory, black smoke started pouring out of his engine.

Then the engine stopped.

"No!" Charger screamed in frustration.

A hush fell over the fans in the grandstands. They all stood up, holding their breath.

On top of the IMP, Jack, Libby, and Duck stared at the smoke coming from Charger's car in disbelief.

"His engine overheated," Duck said. "It shut down automatically!"

Charger's racer coasted to a stop. The smoke pouring out from under the hood thickened, trailing off into the sky. For a long moment, Charger stared at the cloud of smoke, imagining that his dreams of victory were floating away too.

Lyle heard the strange hush in the stands, and quickly wiped the impact foam off his windshield. He peered out to see what was going on.

His heart skipped a beat as he saw Charger's car. "He's stopped," Lyle said.

Lyle glanced at his foam-covered instrument panel. There was still a chance . . .

He pressed the starter button.

Brrrrrrrrmmmmmmmmmm!

Amazingly, Lyle's engine turned over and started up with a roar.

Charger quickly climbed out of his smoking car. He pulled his helmet off and tossed it aside. Then he rushed around to the rear of the racer.

Lyle's wheels screeched as he took off, fighting to keep the battered car in a straight line.

Without a moment's hesitation, Charger braced himself against the back of his car.

He began to push.

Very slowly, the wheels started to turn. Charger's car began to roll toward the finish line.

Charger strained against the racer with everything he had. He'd heard Lyle's car start up again, but he couldn't spare a single second to check back to see how close Lyle was coming. He had to push. Charger thought about nothing else but rolling his car toward the finish line.

All the fans in the stadium were on their feet now, stomping in rhythm. "Push! Push! Push!" they screamed.

Vvvvrrrrrrrrrroooooooooooommmmmmmmmm!

The roar of Lyle's car drowned out the crowd.

Charger let out a sharp groan. The pain in his back from heaving against the heavy car was terrible.

The Collector was coming closer and closer. . . . Charger could hear Lyle's car—and it sounded like it was almost on top of him! The finish line was so close—but Charger's strength was giving out . . .

With a last gasp of effort, Charger pushed the nose of his car over the finish line.

The video screen changed to show a checkerboard flag!

Lyle zoomed past . . . but he was too late.

Charger stumbled to his hands and knees behind his car, totally exhausted. He was so tired, he might have dropped right off to sleep—but the deafening noise of the cheering crowd was too loud.

25

*C*harger stood in the center of the Motorsphere with a crowd of TV cameras circling around him. In his hands he held an oversized check—his first place prize money. Flashbulbs popped from every direction.

Mike Hauger stepped up to Charger. "How do you feel, Charger, after winning the very first NASCAR Unlimited Series race," he asked, "and becoming the third generation of the McCutchen family in the winner's circle?"

Charger smiled. "I feel proud," he replied. "Proud to be a part of Team Fastex."

Nearby, Stunts and Flyer watched Charger being interviewed with big grins on their faces. Suddenly, Flyer noticed someone pushing through the crowd, and his smile faded.

"Glorie," Flyer whispered.

Glorie saw Flyer and gave him a shy smile and a little wave.

Flyer rushed toward her.

"Hey," Stunts called after Flyer. "Ask her if she's got a sister!"

When Charger was done with his interview, he hurried over to Stunts. "You lost your chance to win the race when you helped me, Stunts," Charger said. He handed Stunts the oversized check. "I think you ought to have this."

Stunts opened his eyes wide as he took the check. "But . . ." he began, "but that's your *prize money*, man."

Charger put his hand on Stunts's shoulder and squeezed. "You'll know better what to do with it than I would," he said.

With that, Charger walked quickly away. For the first time in his life, Carlos Rey was speechless.

On his way out, Charger passed Zorina, Diesel, Hondo, and Lyle, who glared at him. "Next time, Charger!" Lyle warned.

Charger ignored them all.

Meanwhile, Stunts was frozen in shock, staring at the big check. He just couldn't get over Charger giving him the money. It was probably the coolest thing anyone had ever done for him in his life.

The Fizz vice-president sauntered over to Stunts and put his arm around Stunts's shoulders. "So,

Carlos," the Fizz VP asked, "can we announce you're going to drive your next race for the Fizz team?"

Stunts shrank away from the Fizz VP and took a deep breath.

"I think I'm already part of a team," Stunts replied.

Then Stunts strode away . . . before he could change his mind.

Over by a table piled with food, Duck was stuffing his face. Next to him, Megan stood with her parents.

"Why don't you have a nickname like the other drivers?" Libby asked Megan.

Megan glanced at Jack. "Maybe a nickname's something you've got to earn," she replied.

Jack smiled. "If that's true," he said, "you've earned it." He handed Megan a cap. On the front of the cap the words TEAM FASTEX were printed in big letters.

Shyly, Megan took the cap and slipped it on.

"Welcome to Team Fastex, *Spitfire*," Jack said.

"Spitfire," Libby said to Megan. "I like it. It suits you." She hugged her daughter tightly.

Out of the corner of his eye, Jack noticed Garner Rexton slinking away. "I'll be right back," Jack told his wife and daughter.

Jack hurried to catch up to Garner. "Garner!" he called.

Garner stopped beside the exit and looked at Jack. "What?" he asked.

"I'm signing over the team owner prize money to

118

you," Jack said, "as the first payment on my loan."

"I'm afraid that's not enough," Garner replied coldly.

Stunts stepped up beside Jack and held out the first place prize check. "What if you add this to it?" Stunts asked.

Garner stared at the oversized check, narrowing his eyes.

"It's enough," Garner answered finally. "For now." He took the check and smiled. "I'm glad you could make the payment, Jack."

Libby walked up and joined the group. Garner nodded curtly to her—the woman who had forever broken his heart.

Garner swallowed and turned back to Jack. "You don't know how happy it will make me," he said, "when we're finally even."

Jack put his arm around Libby, and steered her back into the crowd.

As soon as they'd walked away, Garner dropped his smile.

His eyes glittered cold and hard, like ice.

In the middle of the crowd, Charger held his winner's trophy high in the air. "Let's get charged, Team Fastex!" he hollered. Everybody whooped and cheered around him.

Off to the side, Flyer held out his hands to Glorie. "I wasn't sure I'd ever see you again," he told her softly.

"I'm here," Glorie replied. "It's so good to see you again, Sharp."

"Let's get a team picture!" Charger shouted.

Flyer glanced at Glorie, wondering if she'd be mad if he joined the team photo.

Glorie smiled. "Go on," she told Flyer. "I'll wait."

Megan, Charger, Stunts, and Flyer lined up in front of the huge Team Fastex logo hanging on the wall. All of them wore their TEAM FASTEX caps, and put their arms around each other as they faced the cameras.

Nearby, Miles and Mrs. McCutchen watched the team setting up the picture. "You think I'll ever be a hero, Mom?" Miles asked.

Mrs. McCutchen looked down at her young son. "You're a McCutchen, aren't you?" she replied.

Miles flashed her a giant grin.

Team Fastex had finally gotten set up in the pose they wanted.

"Don't forget to smile!" Stunts hollered.

Flashbulbs exploded all around them, shining on their smiles.

They had plenty to smile about, after all.

Now that they were a real winning team, there was nothing Team Fastex couldn't do!

120